Nothing
But Your
Memories

YOUNG
Writers
CONTEST

The BookLogix Young Writers Collection

Attack at Cyberwold

Messages from the Breathless

Rapunzel: Retold

Thieves of the Flame

Nothing
But Your
Memories

H. B. Clementine

***BOOK*LOGIX**
Alpharetta, GA

10 9 8 7 6 5 4 3 2   1 1 1 4 1 4

ISBN: 978-1-61005-537-6
Library of Congress Control Number: 2014920352

Printed in the United States of America

♾ This paper meets the requirements of ANSI/NISO Z39.48-1992 (Permanence of Paper)

ACKNOWLEDGMENTS

First and foremost, I want to thank Brittainy Crisp, my amazing unofficial editor. She was the one who read the story in its early stages and helped me sort the good ideas from the really, really bad ones. Also, all the members of my family, who are creative and inspiring, and forgave me for spending half the summer locked up in my room writing. I would also like to thank BookLogix for putting out this amazing contest to help give young writers a chance to succeed in the publishing world. Without a deadline and a purpose, I likely never would have finished my book at all, not to mention have the chance to actually see my story in print.

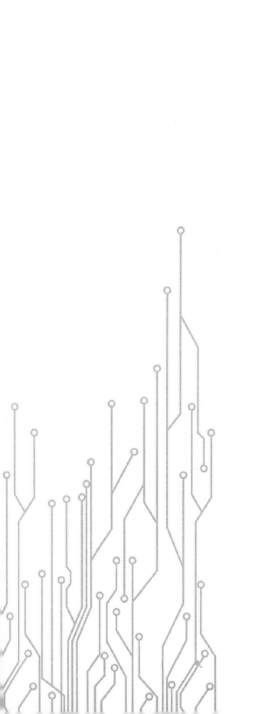

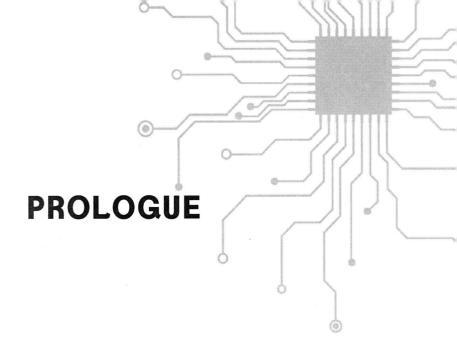

PROLOGUE

They said they were saving the world. Wait, no. They said they were saving us, the people. All those who were crippled, sick, or even dying could be saved. Over and over again, we were told that this was the end result. Who would put down this perfect plan that could save the lives of millions? No one. It figures, right?

Dr. Elrich Simon was the first to coin the idea that your memories are all you need to "be yourself." Over time, the technology was developed to pull all the memories from a person's mind into a small identity chip using a memory dock attached to the neck, leaving an empty shell of a body behind. This chip, along with the original memories, could then be transferred to a new body.

All the reviews and reports of this procedure came through as supportive; after all, there were so many good applications for this technology. But what no one saw was that at the same time one person's life was being preserved, another was being destroyed. Behind the veil of this miracle invention was the silencing of the minds of millions. As one person's memories were taken out of the diseased or crippled body and thrust into a new one, the former occupant was silenced, forever. Memories of their lives were gone, pushed out by the new thoughts of another.

In the early stages of the MB Transfer, the "new" bodies were obtained from insane asylums. The rationalization behind this was that the memories of the "donor" were already so diseased and corrupted that the body was an empty shell to begin with. As cruel and evil as this practice was, no one blinked an eye. Only the benefits were seen.

The first major and recorded unjust use of mind-body transfer was in the War of 2146. A key strategizing officer, General Ray Mandin, and several troops crashed in enemy territory outside a small, rural town, and the general had been fatally injured. Few saw the crash; however, one curious teenage boy from the village snuck out to investigate on his own. The troops jumped him and, using the army-supplied emergency MB Transfer dock, took the general's memories and pushed them into the mind of the native boy. The death of this boy became the symbol of cruelty and injustice. The troops tried to defend themselves by saying that the life of General Ray Mandin was worth the death of an insignificant nobody.

A debate soon arose over whether or not the mind-body transfer, or MB Transfer, was ethical. One would be surprised how long it took for this question to arise, but once it did, in the year 2149, a full-scale revolt broke out. Facilities dedicated to developing and advancing the technology were destroyed. Society was pushing for change—for justice—but by this time the MB Transfer was such a common practice that the change could not be reversed. Doctors in hospitals everywhere fully integrated the use of the transfer into their practices. Even prison wardens were using this technology to put dangerous criminals into partially crippled bodies so that they would be less of a threat.

The MB Transfer was everywhere. Yet, the people would not relent. There were strikes, walkouts, and even straight-up threats against the government to pass a law prohibiting transfer into an already occupied body. Finally, after a long three years, a solid step forward was taken. Scientists Richard Calvin and Dr. Holly Rushweld discovered a way to grow bodies with no memories. These shells, as they came to be known, could have someone's memories imported and then function as any other human would. This was the breakthrough everyone had been waiting for. Life soon returned to a normal state.

Everything seemed perfect for a time, but with this new progression of technology, the population began to grow rapidly, more quickly than any other time in history. Elderly people would continue to buy new, younger bodies, and the sick could also receive a transfer. By this time, about a third of the population lived in shells with a dock permanently installed on their neck. The death rate had become so low that it was almost rare to hear of someone dying.

The first law to try to slow the population growth raised the price and tax of living in a shell. It wasn't enough.

Other laws were passed with few substantial results, until finally another major step had to be taken. A reporter named Rosie Wattes jokingly stated in an article about the population growth that we should all just take turns living. It is debated whether or not this was actually the first formal mention of the idea, but it was certainly the most notable.

Soon after Rosie's joke went viral, a group of scientists wrote out a full, in-depth plan of how the world—or at least part of the world—could actually go into an alternation of generation state. Cities could be developed that allowed for an annual MB Transfer of the entire population of the city. Half of the population would lie dormant with their memories stored on chips in vaults on "sleep mode," where memories are neither made nor destroyed, while the other half would live normally for a year. At the end of each year, the chips of those who had been "awake" would be taken out of the docks and put into sleep mode. The chips of those formerly on sleep mode would then be inserted into the docks of the same shells that had been used the year before and activated so that they could live for a year and continue to make memories. As bodies got too old to be used, they would be disposed of and replaced with shells developed through the Calvin-Rushweld method. This would theoretically allow the population growth to end without the loss of life.

It was a radical plan, but the world needed radical at that point. The population was out of control, and something needed to be done immediately.

A trial run of the Alternation of Generation city was set up and run for six years. Those in the city reported feeling fine after the annual MB Transfer. One young adult enthusiast stated, "It feels like taking a long nap once a year. You wake up a little disoriented because of the time passed, but after a day or two, everything returns to normal."

Before the six years were fully completed, seven other Alternation of Generation cities were in production. Just two short years after the trial run had been declared a success, almost sixty-five percent of the population had a dock installed with their memories stored entirely on an identity chip and were either already living in an AG city or registered to move into one within the next six months.

These cities became safe havens. They were free of the incredibly packed streets and overcrowded apartment buildings. The peaceful communities were almost entirely self-reliant, and there was little contact with those in other cities. As people moved into the tight-knit, closed communities, they reported feeling closer to their neighbors and happier all around.

About three years after the initial rush, the government, which was contained in one of the few non-Alternation of Generation cities, passed a law that required all people not a part of the administration to live within an AG city. The government then assigned a date when everyone who did not already have a dock and an identity chip would go to a predetermined location to undergo the quick procedure to have them installed. After that, each family member would be directed to move to one of the cities and begin life as an AG citizen.

And on that warm Saturday in July of 2161, the Shift was completed, and we would learn to live our lives one year at a time. We had to.

Or did we?

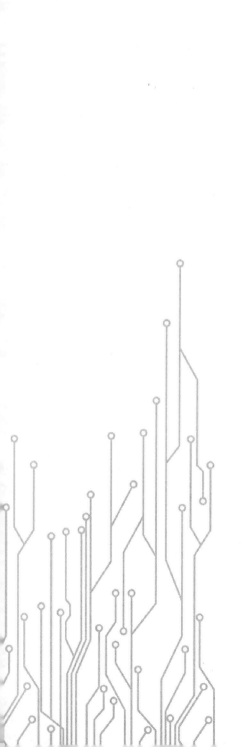

CHAPTER 1

I knew it. As I lie on a white bed in a white room with white light filtering in through the shade on the window, I know it has finally happened. The Shift is complete. As soon as I open my eyes, I regret it. I wish I could just go back to sleep.

"I'm awake," I say aloud into the plain, disgusting, utter whiteness of the room.

I don't know why I'm so opposed to the idea of being an Alternation of Generation Citizen. Maybe it's a sense of pride that I somehow deserve to live in my own body for all the years of my life. Maybe it's a sense of resentment toward those who forced me to do it, but I shouldn't be angry. After all, I am nothing but my memories.

Ha! That crap, I think to myself. *What is that? That's what they told us over and over again as we prepared for the Shift.*

"No, you don't need your bodies; it will be better this way. Your bodies don't define you; you are your memories."

I remember those hated words with perfect clarity. That idiotic look on the Shift supervisor's face when . . .

No.

"No," I say aloud with resolution. "This is my chance to forget all that. This is my chance for a new beginning."

Oh gosh, now I'm quoting lines from the Shift advertising campaign. I'd better get out into society before I lose my mind.

I rise up out of the bed and look around for the touchpad on the wall. It controls the color scheme of the room and allows you to customize your space any way you want. I remembered seeing the touchpads for the first time when I toured the city before the Shift. My dad thought it would be good for my family and me to see what it would be like, to know what we were heading into. I remember walking through rooms like these and marveling at all the amazing technology and the abundance of space.

"These touchpads allow you to change the entire look of your room. With a touch of a button you can make your bed blue and your walls pink." The tour guide then laughed one of those I-don't-really-think-this-is-funny-but-it's-my-job laughs as my dad asked his fiftieth question.

"Do we really get one of these huge apartments each?" I could tell that he was still reeling at being able to have one of these massive rooms all to himself. His amazement was understandable, of course, because our former living quarters had been comprised of a cramped apartment in a thirty-story building that our family of five shared with another family of four. Life there was hard, but we were together, and no one was trying to tell us that we could only live one year out of every ten. You see, at first AG cities had two groups that alternated every year. However, as time went on and more space was needed, the cities began to switch over to three groups, then four, and eventually as many as ten. Oh, and another fun perk of the Shift? No families; everyone functions on their own. Members of the same family might not even be placed in the same generation.

In the city known as The Fisk, where I was fortunate enough to wake up, we have the max number of rotational groups at a total of ten. Yup, I get to live one out of every ten years. Aren't I living life to the fullest? And not only that, but I am in the tenth, or J, rotational group. I'm not really positive why that irritates me—it shouldn't matter—but I guess it makes me feel like I am missing out on a lot. I wonder if AG citizens were supposed to dwell on the nine years of life they are missing out on. *Doubt it.*

Yet, I don't think the AG system itself is inherently bad. My anger stems from not having a choice in the matter. Whether I wanted to or not, I had been shipped off to The Fisk. Maybe one day, had the Shift not been required, I would have moved to an AG city on my own. But, because the Shift is required for everyone, I didn't even get to pick my poison. The city of my future was chosen for me by some sorting computer that placed me and everyone else.

Part of me begins to wonder if there was any sort of evaluation to figure out where each citizen would fit best. The thought comforts me a bit. Perhaps then the middle-aged Mr. Bire, who had formerly lived two doors down from me, will end up in a city near the coast due to his avid love of fishing. And maybe, just maybe, the elderly Ms. Gwendolyn will finally be able to live somewhere warm enough that she won't have to carry a blanket draped around her shoulders at all times. Nostalgia sweeps through me again. I doubt I will ever have the same relationship with my new neighbors as I had with my old ones.

A sudden yearning for human company and a feeling of fleeting time shake me out of my stupor. I quickly locate the room designer touchpad and choose a bunch of colors at random. My new room sports yellow, orange, purple, green, and about any other color you could imagine. It looks like a rainbow threw up on it, but at least it is no longer white. Not ideal, but my impatience to go out and see other living people is suddenly overwhelming. I run over to the closet and pull out the first things I see, rapidly discarding the obnoxious white pajama-like clothing I woke up in. Without so much as a second glance to see what I had put on, I dash out the door to face the new world.

As soon as I open my door, I discover a flurry of activity around me. All I can see down the long, white halls of the apartment building are doors being flung open as both boys and girls rush out to greet their shiny, new future. A girl to my left looks shell-shocked, pun intended, and a guy behind her looks as though he has tears in his eyes as he takes in the new world. Everyone that I can see wears a different expression. I see ecstatic, teary, cautious, and even confused faces on my neighbors' shells.

When the Shift occurred, memories and identities were stored on the identity chips then carefully transported to mind vaults. After the memories had been safely extracted, the former bodies were examined and deemed worthy or unworthy for continued use. Most bodies had some flaw or another and were disposed of through burning. This only occurred behind the scenes though—can't have people thinking that the new system isn't perfect, now can we? However, a few bodies were decidedly fit for future use. These bodies were taken to one of the AG cities and stored until needed.

But since the vast majority of bodies had been disposed of, the vast majority of people would receive new bodies that had been grown on a shell farm. These bodies were typically between fifteen and twenty years of age—mature enough to fully function and not be debilitating, but not so old that they would quickly expire. They also tended to look fairly similar, brown or blond hair and simple but nice features. These new bodies allowed age to truly be "just a number" since, physically, everyone was within a few years of each other. Parents and children were no more. No one from your past experiences would recognize you, nor you them. As much as I hate to admit it, the one good thing the Shift did, in my eyes, was allow people to start over. Memories aren't erased, but new ones can be formed outside the old relationships. It truly does bring a shiny, new future.

Well, I guess it is time to take advantage of this shiny new future. I take a deep breath and step out of my doorway to join the mass exodus of people pressing to get out and explore the world.

Stepping out into this new world is exciting, not utterly horrible and idiotic, I sternly tell myself as I follow the flow of the crowd toward the elevator shafts. As I look around, I see nothing but bright eyes and hopeful expressions. Maybe it is time to put a positive spin on things. *Well, here goes nothing.* I fix a smile on my face, and for the first time, I actually feel like there is a glimmer of hope for the new life I am heading toward.

Wait, did that thought really cross my mind? All of a sudden, I find myself almost laughing out loud at the fact that I had entertained good thoughts about the Shift.

A huge chunk of the crowd presses into the elevator, and I find myself in the far corner. Loud chatter rises up immediately, and I quickly become the only one not socializing. I decide to take a step forward and introduce myself to some people. There is a girl on my left in a stereotypical shell body with light brown hair and a pretty heart-shaped face. Her eyes are wide as she and another guy share their amazement for what they had seen already. She is wearing an obnoxious pink dress with equally obnoxious pink shoes that make her look like she belongs in the twenty-first century. The moment that conversation ends, she emphatically turns to me, and I take that as my cue to introduce myself.

"Hey, I'm Mira," I say, less than confident but with a smile on my face.

"Hello, dear, I'm Catherine-Grace," she replies with an even brighter smile, somehow managing to show almost all of her pearly white teeth.

I immediately recognize the name to be one from the older generation. Newer names tend to have fewer syllables and are very rarely compound. That, and the fact that she called me "dear" in a rather grandmotherly way, tips me off to the fact that the woman in that eighteen-year-old shell and ridiculous dress is probably not anywhere close to the age she looks. It takes a moment of me just standing there staring at her before I am able to speak again.

With all of my teenage tact, I blurt out, "So how old are you really?" Quite the polite young lady, I know. But you will have to excuse me, at seventeen and suddenly all alone in this vast city, manners are not exactly first on my list of priorities.

After a look of shock passes across her perfect, innocent little face, Catherine-Grace finally replies with a slightly reproachful look, "Well now, that wasn't very nice, was it, dear?"

Oh, kill me now. I have already made an enemy. My first ten minutes as an AG citizen are off to a splendid start. I hardly even know this woman, but within two seconds of meeting her, I have managed to offend her. I suppose what I said wasn't exactly the most polite, but it's not my fault that—

". . . and so of course you have a right to be curious, but there is no need to remind us of the past. I think we all deserve a new chance at life here in The Fisk," Catherine-Grace pointedly says as her words yank me out of my silent, internal rant. She then proceeds to turn her back to me with a satisfied look on her face, as though she made some great point.

As she turns, I study her openly. I even forget my frustration and lack of people skills for a moment. It has to be one of the most bizarre things I have ever experienced. Standing before me is a woman, who knows how old, in a body fit for a teenager who's fresh out of high school. Scary. The tone and inflection of her words make it seem like she should be old and wrinkled with kind eyes, slowly carrying a large tray of homemade cookies to some of her grand-children. Instead, she is moving quickly with sharp and precise movements—without a care in the world or a single baked good in sight.

It strikes me how different things are now. I remember when I was simply Mira Cobbleson, the seventeen-year-old girl in apartment 19M; the tall, fit girl with the strawberry blonde hair who tended to be "rather mischievous and sometimes a wee bit rebellious," in the words of the beloved Mrs. Summerfield who had lived four doors down; the loving older sister to her two younger brothers; the one who had just finished high school with high honors and planned to do something great. I never got a chance to decide what that great thing would be.

The summer after I finished high school, I was poised to take a great leap into a future of hard work and success. I planned to try to start working with an organization dedicated to finding a solution to the population issue, a solution that didn't involve forcing people into the AG lifestyle. That future never came.

I remember the years leading up to graduation. In my sophomore year, the Alternation of Generation trial run was announced as completed and fully successful. During that time, all resources were being dumped into building the new AG cities, and the organization I had dreamed of working with crumbled, along with my hope. Throughout my junior and senior years, my family and I watched the world change before our eyes. We watched cities built, our friends leave, and the town around us deteriorate as its funds were drained. When I finally graduated, half the former occupants of our apartment building moved to one of the new cities. Even the family sharing our apartment moved out. Life in our three small rooms became so terribly lonely without the family that we had shared our lives with for the past seven years.

Despite all the hardship, my family and I had never wanted to move. As our neighbors became fewer, we became closer. We knew that if we moved we would be split apart and have to live our lives separately. You see, life in the AG cities was designed to bring about a whole new lifestyle, and distancing oneself from past connections supposedly allowed the a citizen to move on and adapt more easily. As a family, we decided we would stay in our apartment and enjoy life as it was. As long as we were together, we were happy. As cliché as that sounds, it was true. We were each other's constant, and when the world around us shifted like the sands on the beach, we clung to each other with fierce love and compassion.

But then the Shift came.

The announcement was made in the last week of school before my graduation, with the full force of a hurricane ripping through what hope I had left. I once read that if you have destroyed a person's hope, you have destroyed them. Well, by this point, I had been thoroughly defeated. The announcement was made and broadcasted over and over again. Those hated, despised, evil words would play in my mind again and again as I lay in bed and stared at the cracks and water stains on the ceiling above.

I remember thinking to myself, *This is it; my life is over.*

A few weeks after the original message was sent out, my dad took us all to go visit one of the new cities that we would soon be living in. He had always remained optimistic throughout the ordeal. We toured the grounds, led by an overly peppy tour guide who babbled like an idiot about the shiny, new future we were about to have.

Shiny, new future? Was that a sick joke?

My life was right there in front of me, waiting to be grabbed by my oh-so-eager hands. But I was never able to fully grasp it. Instead, a shiny, artificial, plastic piece of junk was shoved in place of what I wanted. Like a small car hit by a bus hurtling toward it at full speed, my life flew out of my control.

By the time I finally accepted what was happening, it was the official day of the Shift. With heartrending good-byes out of the way and weary and beaten expressions on our faces, my family and the few remaining occupants of our town stepped in line to have docks installed and memories uploaded on fragile pieces of plastic. We already knew that we were being sent to live in different cities. Worst of all, it was my birthday. On the sixteenth of July, I pulled myself up into the line to receive the worst birthday present that could ever have possibly been given.

In spite of all this, I had woken this morning open to the possibility of trying to make the most of my life here. But now, the door has been slammed shut—full force. The memories of my family remind me how much I have lost. Teary eyed, I turn to the mirror on the back wall of the elevator. I see what is expected. The shell before me is of average height with generic brown hair and brown eyes and is dressed in the hideous bold-striped pants and baggy sky-blue shirt I had hurriedly pulled on this morning. It is surreal. I move my left hand a fraction of an inch to see if the person I see in the mirror really is me, and of course, it is. I look almost exactly like Catherine-Grace; even my clothes are as bad as hers, and every other clone on this perfect little elevator in this perfect little world. The sight terrifies me.

Have you ever seen yourself in a dream? Did you experience that fear when you gazed upon yourself from outside your body as though you were some sort of ghost? Do you remember how unnerving and haunting that was? Now, imagine that feeling again, only more intense, so intense that the world is spinning around you as you reel about and struggle to find something that will pull you back to reality. But you can never reach reality, because this is

> Who
>> You
>>> Are
>>>> Now.

All you are, the entire length of fabric sewn together to make you, has been shredded, leaving you with nothing but your memories. Everything that defines and separates you from every other person in the world is now contained on a plastic chip the size of a walnut. What kind of life is that?

I slowly lift my eyes, shifting my gaze to the hard-tiled floor up to my neck. I brush aside my straight brown hair and lock eyes on the invention that started it all. The memory dock, a small, black, square contraption, lies embedded in the soft skin of my, no, *this shell's* neck. It serves its cruel purpose by shoving the contents of the inserted identity chip into the brain of the shell it's attached to. This small device holds my entire being captive in a body that I never asked for.

Why did this have to happen?

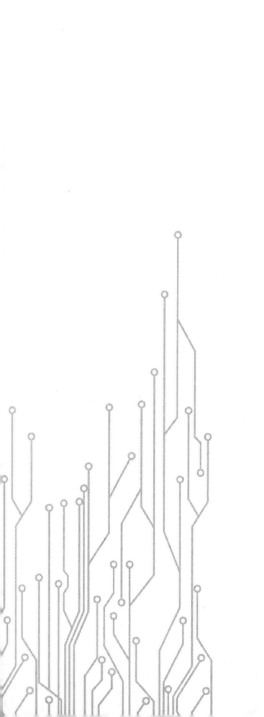

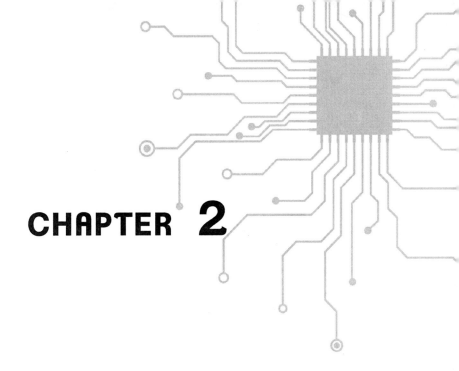

CHAPTER 2

As soon as the elevator finishes its seemingly endless journey from the top floor, I rush out into the gilded lounge and through the doors of the apartment building. I step out onto the wide sidewalk and practically run through the throngs of wide-eyed people to escape. On and on I push to escape something I can't even put into words. I am confused, scared, and furious with the hand of cards life has dealt me. Inside me, there is the fierce desire to fight and resist the change. But opposing those feelings is a longing for life to be peaceful again. I have hardly been awake for an hour, but I am already exhausted from fighting the distress and turmoil within me.

Forget it, Mira! I internally scream at myself. *Look around. There are so many people having fun and enjoying themselves. Why can't you do the same?*

Deep down I know the answer. The Shift is cruel and unfair; but I can't continue letting my anger and frustration keep bubbling up and freaking me out. Right then and there, I vow I will try to adjust to this new life. It isn't fair, and I certainly am not rationalizing the Shift, but I at least owe it to myself to not be miserable. I take a second and slow. I focus on pushing all my fear and anger down into a little box in the depths of my mind. Those same fears and hatreds would find their way out eventually—I know that much—but for now, I had beaten them.

A new emotion comes up from within: pride. Nothing visible from the outside had changed, but on the inside, I had won a battle. The war might not be over, but for today, I resolve to put forth the effort to at least sample this life forced upon me.

My mind stops racing and I slow down. I allow myself to move along with the flow of the crowd for a moment before stepping off the sidewalk in front of Creations Coffee Shop. Surrounding the building are other boutiques and shops with a similar earthy feel. The sight throws me off for a moment. Everything looks so old. Even the name is *so* old-fashioned. I know the AG cities are meant to remind their citizens of another time, but I guess I never realized how completely, authentically old they really are. A glance around shows me that the rest of the city, or at least what I could see, is like the coffee shop.

In the middle of a square, gazing down a broad lane crowded with people gawking at the city, I can see the corner of the apartment building I had fled from. In the other direction, the lane I am on seems to lead closer to the heart of the city, winding its way past shops and bakeries that smell like heaven. Maybe, just maybe, there would be a few things I could like about the city. With a shaky but relieved breath, I square my shoulders and, for the second time that day, fix a smile on my face and walk inside the coffee shop.

When designing the cities, the builders tried to bring back a bit of the past when cities were a little less crowded and there was room for people to sit and talk. Creations embodies that ideal. The place reminds me of pictures from the early 2000s. Comfortable looking chairs in bold patterns dot the majority of the floor space. There is a painting on the wall nearest to me showing scattered shapes in wild colors. It is the kind of bizarre art that had been popular back in the day.

Hanging above the baked goods display, which holds amazing looking cakes and tarts, is a menu written in all sorts of colors and fonts. It is kind of fun to look at. After further examining their menu, which seems to contain every possible baked good and beverage, I decide on a large chocolate croissant and a cup of coffee.

Mouth watering, I step up to the counter and glance around for someone to give my order to. After looking about stupidly for a moment, I direct my eyes down to the counter to see a screen with all of the options available to order. Beside that is a small red finger-print reader with an attached sign that says, "Press Thumb Here To Pay." Slightly abashed for not having noticed the screen earlier, I quickly punch in my order and press my thumb to the reader, marveling as the little scanner records my thumbprint. After the transaction is complete, a little message flashes on the screen. "Thank you for eating at Creations, come again!"

Hmm, perky.

Beside the scanner is a stack of bright yellow flyers that says:

> All Fisk residents are required to attend the informative assembly held in the outdoor theater at 5:00.

I vaguely recall having seen several of those earlier while I was dashing through the city. Beside the notices is a pile of paper maps of the city, and I proceed to pick up one of each, holding the paper and rubbing it back and forth between my fingers. Paper had been more of a luxury than a common item pre-Shift due to the extent of deforestation. Cities had needed to expand and there was nowhere else to go, so the trees had to go. Now there is ample room for trees with the population condensed into the AG cities.

A sudden ding alerts me that my order is ready. I shove the pamphlets in one of my many pockets, then grab my order. While picking up my coffee and stepping over to a small counter to add milk and sugar, I get a sense of déjà vu. My mind flashes back to our old apartment. Every morning my mom would put on a pot of coffee while humming some little tune or another. It became my morning routine to get coffee before doing anything else. Of course, our coffee back then had been made of artificial beans, and we used powdered milk from genetically engineered cows. From what I can smell, this coffee is the real deal.

Hmm, I guess if I have to be stuck here for the next who knows how many years, I can at least take comfort in the fact that the coffee is halfway decent.

I pull myself back to reality in time to stop myself from spilling the milk I had been pouring. (The milk is real too! How nice of those thoughtful, life-stealing government officials.) When I am done, I take my coffee and walk around to find a place to sit. Most of the seats are taken, but a couple tall stools by the window are available. I quickly rush over and snag one.

Sitting there in Creations, I treasure my real coffee and croissant like it was the last food I would ever eat. Every bite I take is like heaven. It is getting progressively harder to hate the city. Looking around, there really is a lot to appreciate. I begin to notice things like the real, living plants growing in every nook and cranny of the shop. Plants had been a rare household sight before the Shift, due purely to the lack of space available to keep them. The water rations had also been too restrictive to provide enough water for anything other than ourselves. But besides the plants, I also notice for the first time how content and peaceful everyone looks. I recall, back before the Shift, that people had been panicked. In about anyone's eyes you could detect a sense of fear. The fact that food prices were rising and apartment rent was getting more difficult to pay had made life scary for everyone. The fear wasn't crippling, but always thrumming behind calm exteriors were wariness and hints of panic.

Now, all I can see in the eyes of those around me is contentment. The two girls over by the other window seem carefree and joyful as they laugh and share stories of their past lives over iced teas, undoubtedly as real as my coffee was. Even the guy by himself on the couch looks happily lost in thought, the coffee in front of him all but forgotten. These people are all in the same situation as I am, and they are really enjoying it. All sarcasm aside, as much as I hate the idea behind the cities, it is becoming increasingly difficult to ignore the beauty of the city itself.

After leaving Creations, I feel joyful and refreshed, probably because of the chocolate and caffeine in my stomach. But, nonetheless, I decide to take advantage of my good mood and take a walk through the rest of the city. I pull out the map from my back pocket and get ready to explore.

I glance down at the map and study it. My apartment building is located at the bottom, the southernmost part of the city, surrounded by five other buildings. Together, the group is labeled as the Royal Oaks Complex. There is another cluster of apartments, the Lincolnton Complex, in the northeastern corner. About halfway in between the two complexes and a bit to the west is the picture of the white stone city hall. In front of City Hall is a fountain and the square, making up the heart of the city. A massive library takes up the entire block to the east of the square, and south of the lake in the far west, is a picture of a massive outdoor theater. This is where the assembly will take place tonight. On one side of the square is the tallest building in the city, "The Garden Clock Tower." From what I can tell from the image on the map, it seems to be less of a building than a steel structure filled with levels of gardens open to the elements and topped with a clockface that looks out to the north, south, east, and west.

I wonder if I can see the tower from where I am. Looking up from the map, I catch a glimpse of it around the corner of Infinitive Clothing Store. All sorts people are mulling around the storefront gazing longingly at the goods they cannot yet afford. I don't quite understand what is to be desired about a shoulder-spiked red and an orange-striped satin top, but hey, to each her own. If an outrageous shirt gives you some sort of goal to work toward, then I suppose that's a good thing. In fact, that is probably a key part of the AG lifestyle—tangible, achievable goals.

Until that day, I couldn't have cared less about my future. I hadn't wanted to care. I wanted to hope that if I ignored the Shift it would go away, but I suppose a change of heart can happen to anyone. It is a hard pill to swallow, but it feels good. Now that I have seen some of the city, I don't feel like I have been given such a sorry lot. It seems like few expenses had been spared in building The Fisk. The more I see, the more I want to learn about my new home.

I follow the road I am on, which does indeed lead to that center square. I pass massive department stores, restaurants, and art galleries, all designed in the style of days long gone. I pass under a leafy vine-covered veranda outside the square that causes the bright sunlight to break into a thousand little spots dappling the ground. While under there, I hear something I had only heard in films—a birdsong. After searching around for the source of the sound, I see a little brown bird twittering away in the nook of one of the support beams. Beneath it is a cluster of twigs. I, well, my shell anyway, am not tall enough to peek inside the nest to see if there are any eggs, but the bird alone is enough. If the bird chose to make its home here, maybe I could consent to living here as well.

I continue into the square. The first thing my eyes are drawn to is the clock tower directly across from me. The steel structure soars above me, and I gaze in awe at the greenery spilling out from each floor. I see people milling around under the first level, and in one corner a staircase that leads to the levels of gardens. I walk across the square as quickly as I can without looking ridiculous, skirting around the fountain and climbing the stairs up to the first level. The plants are all spilling out over the rims of their gargantuan pots. I walk to the vine-wrapped guardrail that gazes over the square.

Another girl comes up beside me. She has blonde hair with a slightly reddish tint. She reaches over to the apple tree branching out beside her, picks one of the bright, red fruits, and takes a bite. We both just stand there leaning on the railing, looking out over the square for a few minutes before she turns to me with a thoughtful look and says, "I think we are really going to like it here." Then she shoots a smile at me and wanders away.

I follow her example a little while later. Apple in hand, I walk back down the stairs and cross the square under the noon sun. City Hall to my right looks imposing with its white pillars and massive doors. In front of me, though, the library looks inviting. The dark lacquered wood doors are propped open as people amble in and out. I don't really feel like reading at the moment, so I continue walking aimlessly. I take a different path than the one I had taken before and continue to explore for the rest of the afternoon before arriving at the Lincolnton Complex to sit and relax. I sit on a swinging bench until the clock tower reads four fifteen and head back toward my apartment to get ready for the assembly.

What I saw during my venture really amazes me. Spaces are wide and open. Stores aren't crammed on top of each other but are instead sprawling over large areas. Buildings are made of brick, stone, and even real wood. Food is all real, and I had not seen any of the EMRs (Emergency Ration distribution stores) which, before the Shift, sold the cheapest bulk food to the truly desperate. And trust me, only the truly desperate would ever voluntarily shop there. The food had often been rancid and months expired, but here in The Fisk, I see nothing but real, delicious, mouthwatering food. I see food that reflects the countries and ethnicities of the old world. I stand gawking in a square where there are restaurants selling food from every corner of the globe.

I had learned so much that afternoon. First and foremost, I realize the beauty and paradisiacal feel of the whole place. There are bushes, trees, and flowers everywhere. The city is clean and fresh-looking, not at all the dumpy pit my pre-Shift mind had imagined it would be. I see lush parks, advanced technology, and unique architecture all seamlessly intertwined in a beautiful display. The city itself is flawless.

As I walk back to my apartment, my mind is still reeling at the realization of how different this life will be. No more dangerous streets, leaking ceilings, power outages for days at a time, or food and water that was better suited for the rats that had infested our home and school.

At the same time though, my family is gone. Why doesn't anyone else seem affected by this? I miss telling my brothers stories to help them fall asleep when the sirens were blaring all night long. Or helping them figure out how to do the homework given to them by evil teachers who loved to torture us. My youngest brother, Cane, always struggled with math and therefore hated it with a passion.

"Cane, you're gonna get through this," I told him with as much conviction as I could.

"Nooooooo, I'll never get it!" Cane had replied as he slumped back in his chair. "Mrs. Mooridge *hates* me. I could get a hundred on everything through the *entire* year and I would somehow still end up failing the class."

"That's not true," I said, although I knew it was possible. Mrs. Mooridge was more fit to be a drill sergeant than a third-grade teacher.

I had glanced around the room hopelessly as he sighed as loud as physically possible. We were working in the room my brother shared with our other brother. The cracked beige walls and equally decrepit desk we worked at were not exactly inspiring genius in me or my brother.

"Come on, try it. This can't be any worse for you than it is for me." I said, trying to get him to sit back up and get through the work.

"I would rather die," he moaned overdramatically, putting his hand to his forehead to enhance the effect.

"Gahhhhh, Cane!" I said, throwing my arms in the air and Cane moaning all the louder. I looked over at him. Khaki overalls covered his hand-me-down T-shirt that may or may not have once been white. Both of our resolves were cracking.

"Can I bribe you with something?" I asked in a last-ditch effort.

"Hmm," he replied thoughtfully, as I raised an eyebrow, "I'll do it for a bajillion cartons of ice cream." He looked up at me slyly.

I knew exactly what he was up to. He knew that we had a bit of ice cream left over from our father's birthday, and he was trying to get me to let him have it without asking directly. The little sneak. I was weak by this point though. I was tired of having to beg him to do the work, and he knew it. He saw the look in my eyes and pumped his fist in the air.

"I love you, sissy!" he proclaimed, leaning over to give me a hug before running into the kitchen to get a spoon and the carton. I rolled my eyes.

"You little brownnoser," I yelled after him. He was such a goof.

I limited him to a small spoonful per correct answer when he got back and watched amazed as he blazed through the work. He probably played me. *Oh, Cane.* It was the little stuff like that that hit me most of all. Those little quirks and family moments that I wouldn't ever get again.

I miss my family more than anything, but I realize something as I walk alone back to the Royal Oaks Complex. There isn't anything I can do about it. It almost hurts to admit it, but I have no way of finding them and trying would only bring trouble. My dad had always said happiness is what you make it. He would want me to move forward and take advantage of this new life. I know that, like Cane, I should try to take advantage of the possibilities in front of me.

Fine, I think. *I suppose it couldn't be too bad to be happy.*

When I reach the complex, I glance around for a moment. The buildings look very similar. *Hmmmm, which one is mine?* I ask myself, trying to decide between two in the center. Going off luck, I hope that it will be the left one. I stride up to the entrance and into the lounge, which luckily, looks very familiar. I head to the elevator and am faced with a new dilemma, which floor is mine? I figure it has to be one of the top ones, because the ride down had been pretty long, so I head up to the top floor to see if I can figure out which one is mine.

I remember that my room had been toward the end of the corridor directly across from the elevator. I stride down the hall, and when I think I am in the general vicinity of my room, I start pressing my thumb to the scanner on each of the doors, hoping that I will soon hear a lock click. No such luck comes on that floor, though I test about twenty doors. I ride the elevator down a floor to floor five. Again, I press a thumb to each of the scanners on the doors I think could be mine until I finally hear a click and go into my room. *That took way longer than necessary*, I internally gripe. Stupid look-alike generic doors. I don't deserve this kind of struggle. You would think that the AG designers could have given the place a little more character. How much white are we supposed to be able to take?

At moments like these, it is so easy to joke about the AG lifestyle with myself, like it is normal. Normal people in normal cities have normal struggles like getting lost. The humanity of the situation brings me fully back to earth after a day of ups and downs. It feels good to have to work to find my door, like maybe I would get to work for a few things here. That would be fine by me.

Finally back in my room, I realize I have little time left. The assembly starts in less than twenty minutes, so I turn to the wall on my right and say clearly and audibly, "Mirror." The wall's tiny scales, used to reflect color, shift and turn to form a mirror along the entire length of the wall. I do a little dance in place for a second. I had known the room could do that beforehand, but it looks so cool seeing it for the first time. Childish moment over, I look at the image before me. The girl that scared me this morning is now a bit more familiar. This body isn't my own—not yet—but after a few months maybe, just maybe, I could get used to it.

My shell isn't ugly. In fact, it could even be considered pretty. Yes, it is stereotypical and generic, but hey, at least the normal isn't ugly. We aren't forced to go around looking like trolls, an interesting and kind of funny comfort. I finally step back from the mirror and turn to my closet. My striped pants and sack of a shirt fly into the corner as I discard them. I have seen what other people do with their "unique," for lack of a better word, wardrobe and now have a better idea what to do. I pull out a bright red skirt that is folded and pleated in all sorts of different ways and a ruffled yellow shirt that is longer in the back. Finally, a dark blue jacket made of a silky, baggy material to go over it all. Turning back to the mirror I see myself in a bizarre outfit that I never in a million years would have worn back home. I laugh at myself. It is a good kind of bizarre, I hope.

I'm officially turning into a new person. What did they do to me? I used to never care about how I looked, my sarcastic side thinks as I shut the door and turn toward the elevators. But even though there is a hint of bitter irony in my words, I smile because it is time to move on.

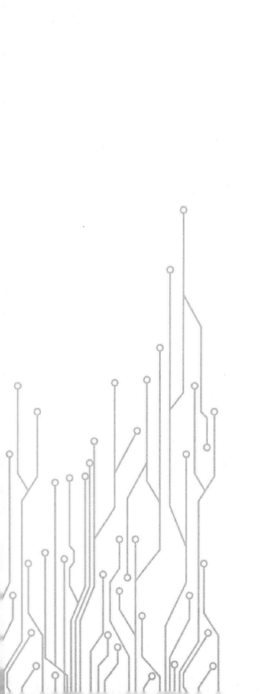

CHAPTER 3

On the way to the assembly, my mind drifts back and forth between a love for the new city and a longing for human conversation. Most of the people I see on my way are in groups of two or three, while I am walking solo. I suppose I haven't really invested much time into making friends, with the exception of the elevator incident and the girl on the clock tower, but as I watch pair after pair of newfound best friends walk past, I feel a prick of loneliness. *I'll socialize tomorrow*, I promise myself as I near the arena. I round the final bend when suddenly my thoughts are cut short by a wave of sound crashing over me.

Hundreds, no, thousands of voices roll over me. When I finally step up into the outdoor arena, I stop and gape in sheer wonder at the number of people there. I can see row after row of AG citizens who all look the same from this distance. It is like staring at a sea of clones. I am paralyzed from shock. The little box in the back of my mind threatens to break apart.

No. This isn't happening. Not here. Not now.

I refuse to lose it in front of all these people. I tell myself it is time to move on, and that hurling at the sight of anyone in a shell would not be a promising step forward. Averting my eyes from the nausea-inducing crowd, I search my vicinity for an available seat. When I finally spot one toward the center of an aisle, I rush toward it and quickly sit down, ignoring the many cries I get from stepping on toes. Immediately, I focus on taking deep breaths to calm myself. *Inhale.* As I sit there, I rationalize my fears. *Exhale.* Of course, there are tons of people here; the entire city is required to attend. *Inhale.* And it's only logical that they would all look similar—the majority of them are in shells—but that doesn't mean they aren't individuals. *Exhale.*

"Excuse me, are you all right?" asks a guy to my right with light blond hair and a concerned expression.

"Oh! Uh, yeah," I reply, startled by the sudden concern of this random stranger.

"Well, you sounded pretty bad there for a second." He must have seen the deer-in-the-headlights look in my eyes, because he quickly backtracks and steers the conversation away from my near breakdown. "Hey, I'm Will. Um, how are you liking life in The Fisk?" He relaxes back into his seat and gives me a smile. He looks so at ease with everything going on. I try to mimic him as I answer, relaxing my posture and sinking into the soft cushion of the chair.

"Nice to meet you, Will. My name is Mira," I say cheerfully, doing my best to recover and prove that I really was fine. Will seems like a nice guy, and I don't want to scare him off. Although, secretly, I am a bit wary, hoping (fingers crossed) this won't be another Catherine-Grace encounter. Despite my reservation, I answer the rest of his question. "I really like it here. It's different, but a good different," I say, being mostly truthful.

"I agree," he replies with laugh. "But the Shift worked out really well in my favor. I think it saved me a lot of trouble." Will then gestures emphatically with his hands, holding them out to show how much trouble he would have been in. "Actually, I *know* it saved me a lot of trouble."

I laugh along with him, then ask, "What got you in so much trouble?" And curiously await his reply.

"I was the owner of a big manufacturing facility that produced electrical appliances for new apartment buildings. Have you heard of Daley Appliances?"

"Yeah, that was the high-end stuff my apartment building could never afford," I reply with a joking smile. Although it is true that equipment had been expensive.

Will laughs again. "Well, that was who we were producing for. Anyway, I had just signed a deal to produce the necessary equipment for an entire apartment complex that was going up. The deal seemed a bit fishy, but it was too good to resist. You should also know that I am not known for reading through entire documents before signing them. I am a bit too trusting for my own good."

"Well, that doesn't sound good," I say, knowing this was going to be bad.

"Yeah, turns out that it was a fake deal and that I had signed over a portion of the company. Let me say that this company had been in my family since my grandfather bought it and made it into the successful business it was. So I pretty much single-handedly threw out all of his hard work. He was still alive, thanks to the shells, and so I had him, my dad, and the entire company furious and trying to figure out exactly what to do with me."

"Oh my gosh! What happened?" I ask through my laughter.

"Luck," he says. "All of a sudden the Shift was coming and we were signing over use of the remaining facilities to the development of new AG cities. I don't think I was ever even officially fired for losing half the company because everyone was so busy," Will says, laughing incredibly hard at his own fortune. "The Shift pretty much saved me from myself."

I am laughing so hard by this point I almost have tears in my eyes. I am laughing not only at the story but also at Will's laughter, because once he really gets going, his laugh is one of those hilarious ones you simply can't help but laugh at. He keeps having to take big gulps of air so he can continue his seal-like guffawing.

In between rounds, I ask, "Did that laugh come with your shell or is it all you?" Catherine-Grace likely would have found that offensive, but Will laughs even harder.

He finally opens his mouth to reply, but I never get to hear what he was going to say because the stage lights up and the assembly begins.

"Hello, new members of The Fisk!" says a figure appearing on the stage below. His words are amplified throughout the theater by massive speakers mounted on either end of the stage, assisted by smaller speakers that line the metal structure framing the stage. His voice echoes through the many levels of seats. Will's and my laughter is over at this point. Everyone in the theater is enraptured by the man on the stage.

"My name is Anthony Walder, and I am the tenth generation supervisor. I am honored to have been chosen to serve you in this position. My goal is to make the transition to life here in The Fisk as simple and easy as possible. My colleagues and I have made your safety and happiness our personal mission. Of course, with your best interest in mind, we have some rules to help protect you and those around you.

"As you may have noticed, some aspects of life here are a little different than what you are accustomed too. There will be handbooks you can pick up after we finish here that will go into each change in detail, but right now, I am going to outline the major ones. First and foremost, the financial system no longer includes the physical money you used to pay with. We now use a completely electronic banking system that will track paychecks and purchases using your fingerprint. (Yes, shells have different fingerprints.) You will receive monthly account balances, and if you are in any amount of debt, your account will be locked until you have earned enough money to pay off the debt. I can see the startled looks on some of your faces, so let me reassure you, any items bought earlier today are free of charge and will not affect your account balance."

A couple of people begin to cheer at this news. I suppose they are the ones who could already be in serious debt. Anthony takes a moment and smiles. His perfect face and the ridiculously white teeth of his shell can be clearly seen on the giant screens to either side of the stage.

"You are probably also wondering how you are supposed to earn money. I'll enlighten you on this as well. Jobs will not be fixed, and you will not be tied to any one occupation. Most of the basic needs of the city are taken care of by machines, but there is still a lot you can do. Things like gardening and being on event coordination committees will provide great and fun opportunities to earn money. You can sign up for various jobs using the touchpad docked in your room. These jobs can last anywhere from a day to a month depending on the assignment. Take note that you will never be obligated to find work if you have no desire to unless you go into debt. Account information and balance reports can be viewed on your touchpads.

"The next issue I will address is that of cars and transportation. I'm sorry to say this, but there are no motorized vehicles here in the city due to the added complications of licenses and potential accidents. Walking will also help keep our shells in top condition. You can, however, purchase bikes if you want a more expedient way to travel."

There are a few groans at this piece of news. But I, for one, am going to enjoy it. Pre-Shift, traveling alone on foot was incredibly dangerous, and anyone who did was pretty much asking for trouble. I remember back in elementary school when we watched a general safety video that taught us things like stop, drop, and roll. Two of the major points of the film were that we should never leave our homes without an adult, and that we were to stay off the streets as much as possible. The danger was especially prevalent in the parts of town where the street lights where broken and the police rarely came, places like where I had lived. Luckily, I will no longer have to worry about that.

"Finally, there are armed guards stationed throughout the city. You have no reason to be alarmed. They are there for your protection and are mandated, by law, to be posted around the clock. Feel free to ask them any questions you might have because, remember, our purpose here is to make life better for you. They can answer questions and are there to help you should the need arise."

Anthony pauses, clasps his hands together, and gazes over the entire audience before continuing.

"I hope that life here in The Fisk truly is like a new beginning for each and every one of you. This city was built for that purpose. The overpopulation of former generations did not allow for members of society to live life to the fullest. Here, we strive to bring you the best we have to offer. We promise to do our part by maintaining the city and watching over the big picture. In return, you, as citizens, are expected to follow the rules dictated by the handbook and exhibit common courtesy to all of your neighbors here in the city. You can do that, right?"

With those last words, a cheer goes up. The audience stands, clapping and shouting their approval. Anthony Walder gives a final wave and backs off the stage into the wings. His words are nothing special, but the meaning that comes with them is a blessing to everyone. With his parting words, the shiny, new future we were each promised became an official reality. And from the sound of the thunderous applause, it seems that everyone is pretty happy with that.

After the applause dies down, people begin to filter from the theater. I open my mouth to say something to Will before he leaves, but he had already merged into the crowd.

There goes my one friend.

A surge of disappointment runs through me. First Catherine-Grace, then the tower girl, if you count her, then Will. AG citizens really aren't my kind of people.

I wait a moment until the initial swell of people dies down then slowly walk out of the theater. Upon exiting, there are massive tables covered with copies of the handbook. I pick one up and continue my thoughtful walk back to the apartment building. There is much to think about. I have a whole new life to start, but where to begin?

As I walk toward my apartment, I watch the night scene unfold around me. Surprisingly enough, there are lots of people out and about. It is only our first day, but that doesn't seem to be an issue for them.

In various restaurants and stores, I see people talking, laughing, and, in the words of Anthony Walder, living life to the fullest. One group of women I see emerge from a large clothing department, their arms are heavily laden with a large number of shopping bags. Everything looks so fun, and it seems like everyone is enjoying it but me. It's not that I'm antisocial, but to be honest, hanging out with a bunch of random people doesn't really appeal to me.

I have always been more of a one-on-one kind of person. In big groups, I tend to get lost in the crowd. My best friend before the Shift was Lillian Clark; she understood that about me, and she had that same kind of personality. She and her family had been the ones to share our apartment. For seven years, we had gone to the same school, shared the same home, and gotten in trouble together. We both cared about our families and our grades, but we also loved to have fun, even if our fun got us in trouble.

I remember in our sophomore year we decided we were going to get jobs. Well, not so much decided, but our parents told us we needed to. They said we needed to take on more responsibility, and a job was a great way to practice for later in life. A few weeks later, after much grumbling and complaining on our part, we finally found work as assistants to our building's monster of a sanitation manager, Harold. He was evil I tell you. Lilli—my nickname for Lillian—and I ended up doing almost all the work at half the pay while Harold sat around doing nothing. You would think with all the advanced technology available there would be little to do, but our apartment building had been old and couldn't afford the fancy equipment.

Our job involved what were probably the two biggest cleaning tasks in the building—vacuuming and mopping. On a typical day, we would vacuum the crummy carpets in the halls for a solid hour, only to be told it needed to be done again. After round two of vacuuming, we would head down to the lobby to mop the beat-up tile floor. The mopping was one of the most frustrating tasks because no one ever cared enough to walk around the area we were working on. They would walk right through, tracking their mud-crusted shoes all across the floor. It made Lilli and me furious. We would have to drag our buckets up to each of the twenty floors to mop the landings in front of the elevators. This was only marginally better than mopping the lobby because there was less foot traffic. Still, we hated it with a passion.

After our second week of employment, and our millionth mopped hall, Lilli and I decided it was time for some fun. The limited pay and disgusting tasks really weren't working out for us, but instead of quitting, we decided to get fired. It wasn't our finest hour, but it was certainly one of the most hilarious.

We headed to meet Harold one day after school to get our assignments for the afternoon. Earlier that morning, I had borrowed one of my brother's toys, a can of little toy bees that would fly around and buzz like the real thing. They could be rather realistic to someone who wasn't expecting them. When Lilli went to grab our mops and the rest of our supplies, she pretended to not be able to find the window spray. With a grunt about us being thickskulled, Harold lifted his massive body out of his well-used chair and went into the closet to look for the missing spray. I quickly scattered about twenty of the little bees in the corner of our evil boss's office.

After finding the missing supplies, we pretended to head out to start our day's work. We watched Harold enter his office and shut the door. As soon as he did we quietly ditched our cleaning equipment and ran back to crouch by the office door. With a stifled laugh, I hit the button on the remote control that would cause the bees to start buzzing and flying around. Not two seconds after I committed my evil deed, shouts of alarm rose from the office. Harold came bursting through the door as though he were being chased by the devil himself. Lillian and I doubled over and laughed till our sides were sore.

When I finally deactivated the bees, and my accomplice in crime and I had caught our breath, Harold realized what happened. We were promptly fired, and he actually threatened to force our families out of the building. We hadn't thought he would go that far, but Lilli was an astounding actor, and she poured out an apology filled with compliments and seemingly heartfelt remorse. I suppose Harold had not been expecting this display of eloquent wording because, with a dumbfounded look, he let us off the hook without kicking us out of the building. We definitely got lucky that Harold was an easy one to flatter, or the consequences would have likely been a lot harsher. Best of all, our parents never even found out. All we told them was that we had been fired because Harold couldn't afford to pay us any longer.

This was only one of our many crazy stunts as Lilli and I were practically joined at the hip, and were constantly making mischief of some form or another. Just think of all the good-natured pranks you can pull when your accomplice in crime lives with you. That is, until her family moved out. It was the summer before our junior year when her dad announced they were moving. Mr. Clark had been offered a high-paying job in the development of one of the new AG cities, and, of course, he accepted. Within a week, their family moved out.

It is one of the hardest things I have ever experienced, my best friend, practically my sister, leaving me. I never really made any new friends throughout my junior or senior years. I guess I will continue that streak in The Fisk. Saddened by my lack of friends, I trudge back home.

Correction: back to my apartment. My true home had been torn down nine years before.

CHAPTER 4

The buildings begin to thin as I near the complex of apartments. Still moping in self-pity at my lack of friends, I shuffle along at the speed of a snail. All of a sudden, some random guy slams into me, knocking me to the ground.

"Oh my gosh, I'm sorry!" he says as he pulls me to my feet. He has a fearful look in his eyes, and he doesn't even make eye contact as he apologizes. I start to ask him what is going on, but he rushes into a nearby furniture store, leaving me reeling in the street.

"What just happened?" I ask myself out loud, as I stagger about rubbing a freshly bruised elbow. Before I can even start to process the event, one of the armed officials that Anthony talked about in the assembly strides up to me.

"Excuse me, miss. Have you seen, in the last few minutes, anyone that seems suspicious or out of place?" he asks urgently.

Immediately, I think of dashing-through-the-dark guy who had knocked me to the ground. But he wasn't really out of place; he had been, uh, night jogging?

"Well?" the guard asks, growing impatient.

"Oh, uh, no, sir. Sorry," I stammer. I'm not as skilled as Lilli in dealing with situations like this.

"That's all right. Now if you'll excuse me," he replies, rushing over to another girl, presumably to ask her the same thing.

I stand there for a moment stunned at what I have done. I had potentially lied to protect a criminal! Why had I done that? I stand there in shock at my actions. That man could have been dangerous, and I had lied to protect him. I spur myself to a brisk walk toward my apartment. What if the guard came back because he somehow knew I hadn't been completely honest? My life would be over. I have no idea what they do to those who break the law, but I don't want to find out. As mischievous as I had been pre-Shift, I had never done anything like this.

I have to go back and tell the truth.

No, I can't.

It's the right thing to do.

But I don't want to get in trouble on my first day!

I practically begin to hyperventilate as the devil on my left shoulder argues with the angel on my right. They decide to allow a compromise if I go back and check out the guy for myself. He may have just been some random guy who happened to have been at the wrong place at the wrong time, but if he wasn't, I couldn't let him run around the city unchecked. It is a bit of a cliché superhero moment, but I decide to take matters into my own hands.

Relieved to finally have a plan, I spin on my heel and begin to head toward the furniture store I had seen the culprit disappear into. I am assuming that he hasn't left already, which seems like a safe bet. After all, if I were some sort of crook hiding from the authorities, I would probably wait a good, long time to make sure it was safe.

When I make it up the stairs and through the door, I scan the place for my target. Not seeing him immediately, I begin to walk through the rows of couches and bedside tables, careful to keep the door in sight so he couldn't slip out. As I turn a corner into the lamps section, I finally see him. Dashing-through-the-dark guy has his back turned to me and, with a quick glance over his shoulder, disappears into a side room.

This is when you're supposed to accept that it's out of your hands, Mira, I tell myself, as my heart pumps loudly. But something pulls me forward. Maybe it is a desire for adventure—a hint of old Mira rising up again. Regardless of what it is, like a little girl playing spy, I sneak up to the door and press my ear up against it. Nothing.

Whatever mysterious force that is controlling me must be pretty strong because I suddenly find myself twisting the knob to see if it is unlocked. Both to my dismay and excitement, I find that it will open. The smart side of me pushes out one last final attempt at rational thinking before adrenaline takes over. I know it is stupid and probably dangerous—that guard had seemed pretty desperate to find this guy—but I suddenly want to be important. I want to be the one who saves the city from this unknown threat—*stupid superhero syndrome.*

The door slides open silently without any hesitation once I turn the knob. It actually somewhat angers me. Doesn't my savior moment deserve a more dramatic entrance? I don't know why I expect an ominous creaking noise though. After all, this is The Fisk, not some derelict, old ghost town. After chiding myself and, yes, stalling a little, I finally step forward into the side room.

The small space contains, surprise surprise, a few miscellaneous pieces of furniture that are broken or missing parts. I also see a doorway in the right wall and, upon standing there for a second, hear voices coming through it. Not one voice, but several can be heard softly speaking through the opening. I sneak over to the wall, being as silent as I possibly can. I press my back against the smooth surface and lean as close as I dare to the doorframe.

"I almost got caught on the way here. An officer saw me and somehow recognized me."

It is dashing-through-the-dark guy.

"This isn't safe. We need a more secluded meeting spot," says a female voice.

"I agree with Alexis, but it won't help if all the guards are already wary of us," says yet a third voice, a guy this time. Thanks to this guy, I also have a name for at least one of the mysterious group.

"Why are we meeting here in the first place and not in one of our apartments? West? This was your idea," says the girl voice, presumably Alexis.

"I don't know. I thought it was a good idea at the time, but what I don't understand is why that guard was after me." It is that first guy again, West.

"Well, you were one of the ones they had to sedate to have the chip installed, right?" asks Alexis. After a pause and what I'm assuming is a nod, Alexis continues. "Well, if that's the case, then it's possible that the officers have been assigned to keep tabs on you. Did you go to the assembly?"

"No, I have no desire to be one of their perfect little Fisk citizens," says West with a scoff of contempt.

"Then the officials probably noted your absence and sent an officer to find out what happened. How could you have been so stupid?" Alexis suddenly accuses. "Now the authorities are going to be keeping closer tabs on you than ever. We don't want to draw attention to ourselves. We *can't* draw attention to ourselves, if we ever want to leave," she says with emphasis.

"She's right, West. You're going to have to lie low for a while; we need this to all blow over before we can really work on getting rid of the chips and getting out of here."

Wait, what!

They are trying to leave the city? They are going to try to get rid of the chips? This could be my chance to get out of here, to live every year of my life! To not be controlled by a chip docked in my neck. The thought entices me more than anything else I can imagine.

No. No!

I had spent the entire day trying to convince myself that I could be a good Fisk citizen, that I would be happy with the Alternation of Generation lifestyle. I had locked away all of my rebellious and hateful feelings in that little box in the back of my mind. At the moment, that little box reminds me, tearing apart my resolve, that no amount of gardening could ever make up for a real life. Suddenly, my priorities make a massive shift. How did I ever fool myself into thinking I could be satisfied with this life? *There is more to life than a pretty city*, I sternly remind myself. I must have been so shocked by the perfection of the city that I had forgotten to think about anything else.

But, still, it is a pretty city, and safe. No more bullets flying and sirens blaring every night. No longer would I have to worry if I was going to get poisoned by the raw sewage lying around in the streets.

Mira, get a grip. Life was still better then. You're growing soft already.

I try to ignore the nagging reminders about the trials of life Pre-Shift—the perpetual illnesses floating in the air, the random electricity outages, gang threats, the truly awful food. Oh, man, the food was bad.

No. Stop thinking like that.

I saw a way out, and there is no way I wouldn't take it. I no longer want to be a happy citizen here; I want to get out. This rebellious group I stumbled upon showed me the door to a life I hadn't even known was there. I don't know what I would do outside the city, or even how I would survive, but I know I want it. That little box in my head, where I forced my hatred and anger, explodes.

The impact shakes loose all the anger and hatred I feel about the Shift. As the wave of old emotions rises up, it coats every one of my thoughts with a new purpose—escape. In less than twenty-four hours, I have come full circle. I had turned from anger, to acceptance, back to anger, and toward resolve. I know what I want: freedom. The age-old desire that had formed nations, united great powers, and conquered oppression. Cheesy? Yes, I know, but it is true. Well, now it is my turn, but I can't do it alone. I need help, and I know just where to get it.

Without giving myself a chance to chicken out, I rashly stride into the room to greet Alexis, West, and the third mystery guy. I probably should have thought through my plan a little more, because walking into a room with a secretive group of rebels to introduce myself didn't go as well as I had hoped.

As soon as I turn the corner to head through the doorway, their talking ceases. And with a quick panicked look toward Alexis, who nods, West jumps up and puts his hand over my mouth. I try to scream, "I want to join you!" but my cries are muffled by West's hand. Before I can wiggle out of his grasp, the third guy, whose name is still unknown, picks up a broken-off chair leg and smashes it down over my skull.

That went well, is my last sarcastic, coherent thought before blacking out.

CHAPTER 5

"Uhhhhh," I moan. "My hhheeeeeeeeaaaaaaaaadddd."
I am practically swimming in self-pity at this point. It feels like there
is an elephant in my head that is pounding on the walls of my brain
trying to break out. *Well the joke is on him,* I think, *because he isn't getting
out of my head any sooner than I'm getting out of this putrid, stinking city.*

Why did I have to walk in there like an idiot? What was I expecting,
a warm hug as we linked pinkies and made friendship bracelets?
They are a freaking rebel group trying to escape the city in utter secrecy,
and I walked in prepared for smiles and a fuzzy welcome. Instead,
a wooden chair leg had come crashing down over my head.

"Ugghhhhh," I moan again for no single reason. It is more a
moan for the general predicament I am in.

My eyes are closed, and I have no plans of opening them, but
I can tell that I am lying on my side on a carpeted floor. Am I still
at the furniture department in that back room? Had they left me
there? I want to open my eyes and look around, but as naïve as it

is, I feel that if I keep my eyes closed I can sleep away that whole ordeal.

Turning to alternative methods of observation, the light behind my eyelids is far too bright to be coming from that back room. If I recall correctly, there hadn't been any windows in either of the two rooms, so they must have brought me somewhere else. Although my memory of the event isn't the greatest, I am too focused on being an idiot to think clearly. On the bright side, they hadn't dumped me in an alley. How kind of them.

Good to see my sarcasm is still topnotch, even with an elephant pounding from within my skull.

I don't know how long I lay there, but I drift in and out of sleep for a long time before I finally hear a stirring behind me. My sleepy eyes peel open to see what is happening. I can't live in ignorance anymore. Oh well, it had been nice while it lasted.

The first thing I see is a white wall that looks very familiar. The plain color also makes up the carpet I am on, as well as the ceiling. Of course, I'm in an apartment. Now, the question is whose? Well, whoever it is clearly has poor taste because everything is still bland, boring, dizzying white. I start to roll over onto my side, trying to be as silent as possible, but my pathetic spy skills aren't up to their usual caliber because I hit my foot on one of the bedposts behind me and let out a sharp yelp. There goes that plan.

"Rise 'n' shine, it's another wonderful day here in The Fisk," says Alexis, apparently having woken up, her voice oozing cruel sarcasm. I'm not sure exactly what to do, so I settle for sitting up and looking around. The room around me is almost an exact copy of mine, with the exception that everything remains a disgusting white.

"You gonna get up? Or are you going to sit there on the floor like you did all night? We have to go meet Faustino and West and decide what to do about you." Alexis is practically spitting venom at me as she says those words. I remain still and watch her get up out of bed and head over to her closet to grab clothing. I see that her closet is stuffed with the same kind of old-fashioned, flowery,

frilly stuff that my own is. Whoever stocks all the closets has terrible taste.

Alexis's shell looks remarkably unique. She has the same brown hair and eyes that most of us do, but her face is what makes her stand out so much. She is pale with a multitude of freckles, and her eyes are such a light brown that they almost look amber. She doesn't look quite as generic as the rest us.

Well, then, lucky her, I think.

Alexis grabs a new outfit with barely a glance at what she holds. Apparently she doesn't care much for The Fisk style either. After she dresses, she turns to me. I wonder how eyes with such warm color can look at someone so coldly. I feel like a bug under a microscope.

"How did you find us last night?" she asks, her glare still as piercing and angry as ever.

"I followed that one guy, uh, West?" I'm not sure about the name, but it is clear she understands. She nods toward her bed, and I take the cue to walk over and sit down. She stands opposite me, blocking the door. I'm not exactly sure how I am going to pull it off, but I still know I want to join them. They are my chance to escape, and I want that more than anything else. As weird as it sounds, I understand their actions the night before. If I had been in a secret meeting in which I was making a plan to violate the law and some random person walked in, I probably would have hit them over the head with a chair leg as well. No, I don't have Stockholm syndrome, but I do understand where they are coming from.

I need to be a bit more tactful than I had been last night if I want to actually somehow join these people. The girl in front of me continues to simply stand there. Probably trying to melt me with her gaze or something. For all I know she had been a voodoo doctor from one of the anti-technology tribes that we had read about in our history textbooks. It isn't looking promising, but I know that I need to get her to like me, or at least trust me, if I was going to have any chance of joining up with her.

I start to tell her about how much I hate the cities, in an attempt to relate to her, but before I get two sentences out, she gives me a pointed yawn, clearly telling me that she doesn't care at all. So rude, and no change in Alexis's stone cold expression. Okay . . . time to try a new tactic. Kind and relatable isn't working, so maybe it is time for old, rash Mira to make an appearance.

I shift my pleading expression to one that hopefully resembles confidence and a bit of my irritated attitude then firmly say, "Alexis, I don't care if you don't like me, but we are on the same side. You want to ditch this superficial life, just like I do. You can't kill me without drawing too much attention to yourselves, but if you refuse to let me join you, I may have to expose you to The Fisk police."

She starts to say something, but I continue, not giving her a chance to get anything out. "I'm not an innocent little girl, and I am willing to do about anything to get out of here, and if it turns out to be to my advantage to turn you in, then I may have to do that." As I make my threats, I casually glance down and inspect the nails of my shell. They really are rather pretty.

Back to the moment at hand, I glance up the girl across the room from me. *Yeah,* I think to myself, *I can play hardball,* and something in Alexis's shocked expression tells me that she hadn't been expecting that. Her wide eyes give her away immediately. She tries to put back on her I-don't-care-what-you-say mask, but I had already see her shock. I take it a step further.

"And you should know, Alexis, that you and your friends owe me. Without me, you never would have even made it this far."

"What? No, we don't," she replies, still struggling to recover from the revelation that I am not some naïve little angel.

"Oh, yes, you do," I say with a smirk on my face.

"Then do tell me, little girl, why we 'owe' you." With her feet finally under her, Alexis's sharp tone is back, but beneath it, I can still sense a hint of fear.

Using this to my advantage, I try to play up my little stunt with the officer last night. "You see," I say, then take a breath and glance casually around—she is in the palm of my hand. "Last night, I was casually walking back to my apartment after the assembly. When all of a sudden, your friend West ran into me. He helped me back up, but immediately darted into that furniture store. Before I could follow him to find out what was going on, an officer came up to me and asked if I had 'seen anyone suspicious' lately."

By this point, Alexis is practically in shock. She probably thought that I had turned them in and that I had been told to follow West so that the officials could see if he was working alone. I feel like such a bad girl. I laugh on the inside. The tables have turned entirely in my favor. I am completely in control of the situation. I have to be careful though; I can't scare her too much, or I would risk having her think I am not dedicated to leaving the city.

I quickly finish my story. "I stood there before the officer and lied to his face. I told him that I hadn't seen anyone that matched his description, and he headed off to ask others the same question." I can see the tension drain from Alexis's face. But before I lose her completely, I need to drive home my point. This is the time to fully win her over.

"Alexis, I risked having my life here in The Fisk ruined to save you, West, and Faustino. I hadn't even known it at the time, but by doing the wrong thing, I gave myself a ticket to the life I deserve. But at the same time, if you refuse to help me, I do have the upper hand. At any point, I could go to an officer and tell them that I stumbled upon a group of rebels trying to live outside one of the law-mandated AG cities. I really, really don't want to do that, but if you refuse to help me, I won't be able to keep your secret. It's your decision really."

I finish my little speech, which I am really quite proud of, then pause and stare directly at Alexis while I wait for her to respond. Surprisingly enough, she never meets my gaze. Perhaps her tough-girl attitude is an act. Finally, after what seems like an eternity, Alexis responds.

"Fine. I'll see what I can do," is all she said before motioning for me to follow her out the door.

Yes! One down, two to go.

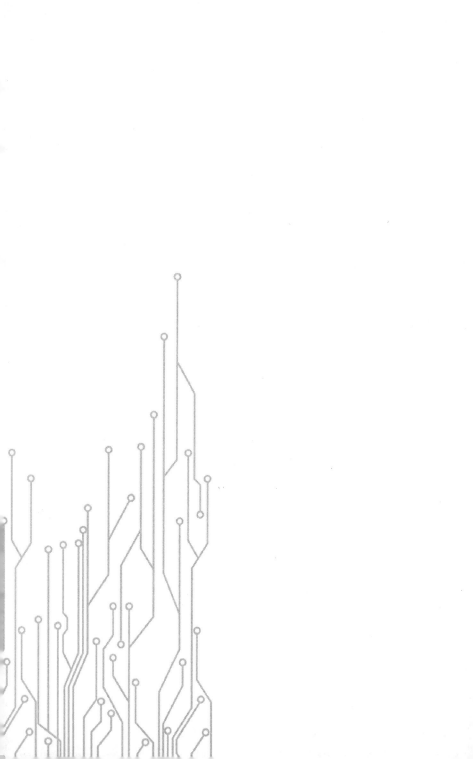

CHAPTER 6

I follow Alexis out of her apartment building, which turns out to be right next to mine, then through the city. I once again see the beauty of The Fisk, but this time it doesn't faze me. I am on a mission now. We see women shopping, guys playing music on street corners, and lots of gardening being done. Gardening is one of the projects you can sign up for to earn money, and it looks like lots of AG citizens are taking advantage of this fun and easy job.

Surprisingly, as high tech as The Fisk was, you never really see lots of crazy equipment. Yes, there is advanced technology, but it isn't overwhelming. No robots doing all the work for us. The city is designed to have people working and occupied, probably so that they won't think about the injustice being done. No one seems to really dwell on that though; the gorgeous vines crawling up trees and the lush parks seem to make up for it. I sigh. This city really is beautiful. If only it were just a city, not an AG city.

I wonder if there had ever been cities like this before the Shift. I would have liked to have lived in one. All the ridiculous amounts of greenery give the city a paradisiacal feel. Not to mention the feeling of the community. Because of the ten-generation cycle, each individual generation is fairly small. There are a lot of people, but not so many that you would feel lost in the crowds. Jobs are designed to help people meet others, and they almost always require a large number of people.

Everything is so open-ended, and it creates the perfect environment for collaboration. If you want to have a massive party at two in the morning where everyone eats oranges and drinks hot chocolate, then by all means, go for it. You could organize a committee and go at it, find sponsors, and make the thing happen. Being able to set and achieve a common goal is an amazing way to bring people together, especially on such a massive scale. The city is like a giant canvas waiting to be drawn on by anyone who is brave enough to pick up a brush and make a difference.

Opportunity before the Shift had been limited. Few ever really got to pursue their creative passions; only the very wealthy could afford to indulge in such pastimes. Even fewer were able to make a living off of them. To survive, most people buckled down and headed into the fray to compete for the same low-end jobs that everyone was vying for. Independent business? Virtually impossible. It was an every man for himself kind of world. But now, there isn't that same level of desperation. No one *has* to get the next gardening job to survive. There are plenty of opportunities for everyone. People are finally able to work with others, not merely compete with them.

All of these different factors allow the community to really get close and feel united. There is even a certain feeling of unity with those who use your shell in the other generations, your shellmates. It is kind of like the shell is important to you and all your shellmates, so you all work together to take care of it, one year at a time. I know I could wake up any year and be significantly chunkier than I have ever been before, if the girl in the generation before me decides she wants to eat five meals a day. I also know I could hack my shell's hair off with a pair of scissors, and my shellmate in the generation after me would have to deal with it.

Oddly enough, this is kind of a comforting thought. Not the prospect of being able to absolutely ruin a person's appearance for the next year, but the idea that we are all in this together. It is comforting in a bizarre kind of way.

All these little things create the feeling that the city is your own little world, literally, considering the fact that you aren't allowed to leave. Ah, there's the rub.

If I had to choose somewhere to spend the rest of my life though, I would certainly pick somewhere like The Fisk. Yet, I dream of leaving, because despite all the fancy flowers, The Fisk is still a prison.

Hopefully, that dream will come true, and the silent girl in front of me is helping me get a little closer to realizing it. We near the other end of town as the sun near the midday mark. When I think about the time I realize I haven't eaten anything but a croissant, some coffee, and the sandwich I had gotten for lunch yesterday in nine years. My stomach suddenly comes to life, begging for the meals it had missed last night and this morning. I am as eager as ever to meet the rest of our little rebel group, but at the moment, I desperately need food.

"Alexis," I said, "I need some food, like, now." I consider asking nicely, but it seems that confidence and bluntness work better with her this morning.

"Sure, sure, but we have to do this quickly; we are meeting Faustino and West at noon," she replies.

We head over to the nearest deli, and I quickly order the first thing I see on the menu. The machine behind the counter quickly puts together my order and the fingerprint scanner notifies me that I will be allowed to purchase the meal, but I would have to pay for it by the end of the week. I note the message then rush to pick up my meal and start eating. I sit there wolfing down some sort of Mediterranean dish that is so good and *real* I couldn't put it in my mouth fast enough. As I eat, Alexis frustratingly watches me.

"Um, are you going to get anything?" I ask her. I feel a little awkward sitting there shoving food in my face while she eats nothing. Not to mention that, technically, I am still sort of a hostage; she is still in control of my fate. Things like that tend to make a meal awkward.

"Not hungry," is her terse reply. Hmm, her loss; the taste of the real vegetables—not the freeze-dried, genetically-modified, nutrient-depleted stuff I had eaten in the past—is so good. I suspect the food will be the single greatest thing I will miss about the city.

"You better eat faster, or we are going to be late," she tells me, avoiding my gaze.

A new urgency stirs within me and a glance at a clock on the wall tells me that it is time to go. I dump the rest of my meal with a sad sigh, and Alexis and I resume our trek through the city.

After a short while, we reach another set of apartment buildings. We walk through the entire city, yet strangely enough, I feel no hint of tiredness. *Must have something to do with the shell,* I think. We briskly walk through the clusters of buildings until we arrive at one of the farthest and most deeply hidden. Still, as buried as it is, it is beautiful, like every other structure in the city. I follow Alexis like an eager puppy as she climbs up the stairs into the foyer. She immediately heads for the elevators. We finally arrive at apartment 7C, and I watch as Alexis knocks on the door. Finally, this is my chance to win a new life. I have to play it right.

One of the guys from the night before—Faustino, I think—opens the door, and Alexis and I step in. The room we are in is almost exactly like mine had been before I changed the colors around. Same white bed, walls, and carpet. It probably reflects the absolute evil of the soul of its owner. Or, you know, something like that. As we did, I look at Faustino. Judging by his name, he is most likely of Hispanic descent, although he looks like any other Fisk resident in his fair-skinned shell. Weird. As soon as we get inside, Faustino shuts the door and turns to us. West is sitting on the bed, and both guys are staring, no, glaring at me. I start to say hello, but Alexis elbows me in the rib.

"How did she do last night?" Faustino asks Alexis from his post by the door. "Did she freak or try to rat us out?"

"I wouldn't be surprised if she's being paid to follow us around and learn all our secrets. You wouldn't do that, little girly, now would you?" West says as he rises up off the bed and heads toward me. "You would never do that. You are going to be a good little girl, or we might have to hurt you. Although, I was planning on teaching you something about listening in on people's conversations anyway." I can tell he is trying to intimidate me and freak me out, and it does, a little. Yet, I don't really feel terrified. My shell is probably defective—I am an idiot at the worst of times and not afraid when a guy in a group of rebels is threatening me.

West starts to raise his hand up in a fist when Alexis stops him with a scoff of contempt. "You aren't going to believe what she told me," she says, giving me a pointed glance.

"What?" says West, lowering his fist and turning to face her. Faustino still remains in the doorway, not saying anything.

"She told me she wants to join us," is all she says.

I watch as the two guys shift their eyes from Alexis, to me, and back to Alexis. West clearly shows his shock with an open mouth as he rubbernecks back and forth between Alexis and me, but his counterpart, Faustino, stands there with a barely raised eyebrow.

We all sit there for a moment in silence, waiting to see who would speak first. I take it as my opportunity to plead my case.

Deep breath.

"Alexis, West, Faustino, you all know me as 'the girl who dropped in on our meeting uninvited.'" I look over at Alexis for approval, and she gives a slight nod toward me. It isn't much, but I take it as a sign to continue.

"But really, I'm like you. My name is Mira Cobbleson. I moved to The Fisk on the day of the Shift. I didn't want to. In fact, right now, I want more than anything to get out of this putrid, stinking city. This isn't my home, this," I say while gesturing at myself, "isn't even my body. West, I lied to protect you, and at the time, I didn't even know why. All I know is that you people are my chance at a real life, the life we all deserve. I can help you. I know I'm not on the radars of the city officials, which could be an asset to you. My dedication is unwavering. I was knocked out, dragged to a strange apartment, and practically held hostage for a night, and yet I still want to join you. Please. I don't want to turn you in. I want to help you, and I'll do anything to prove it to you." I stand there in the silence, waiting to see if what I have done will be enough after all.

"Go wait in the hall while we talk about it," Alexis finally says after a quick glance at her two counterparts.

I head out and stand with my back against the pale, yellow walls. I can't do anything else. If they decide not to admit me, there is nothing I can do about it. I wonder what would happen to me though. Would I go crazy? I'd be forced to live in The Fisk forever. Literally, forever. Ugh. But on the plus side, they do have amazing food. I suppose I could always find a little happiness in that.

Ten minutes later, I am still sitting out there. I am trying to distract myself by making pictures out of the swirly patterns in the carpet. It's funny how suspenseful times like this can actually turn out to be boring. I try listening with my ear to the door, but whatever material it is made of seems to be almost entirely soundproof; I can barely hear anything more than scattered mumbles. I try looking/listening under the door, but some guy comes walking down the hall and gives me a funny look, so I stop with that.

I rediscover the meaning of a minute out there in the hall. All sixty stinking seconds of each minute. The ticks of the gilded, glass-covered clock at the end of the hall become increasingly more annoying as time wears on. I chew at the nails of my shell until they are nothing but nubs. For a moment, I think I hear yelling back in the room, but as soon as I try to listen in, the sound dies away. On and on the minutes drag.

I am amazed at my patience, which has never been a strong suit of mine. I am somehow managing not to bang on the door demanding an answer, like I probably would've done pre-Shift. Perhaps once I am out of here, I can look upon it as a learning experience.

Ha, nope. That would never actually happen, but the stress this place causes me has likely aged me several years. I need to get out quick before I get Alzheimer's. Can shells get Alzheimer's? The bizarre thought leads me to other questions. Can shells get sick? How long can shells live? Are shells even technically human? All of these questions stew around in my head and lead me to bigger ones. I begin to wonder how the Shift ever even happened. Like who exactly is in charge of all this? Who is the one responsible for deciding that everyone should be forced into the AG lifestyle? I don't know who it is, but I don't need to have an immense hatred for them. Who do they think they are? Some sort of god?

My mind spins round and round trying to distract itself with snarky questions it doesn't have answers to, until finally, Alexis opens up the door. "You're in," is all she says. I can't tell whether she is excited or angry with the decision, but I barely contain my excitement. It takes all of my self-control not to jump up and pump my fist in the air.

I am in.

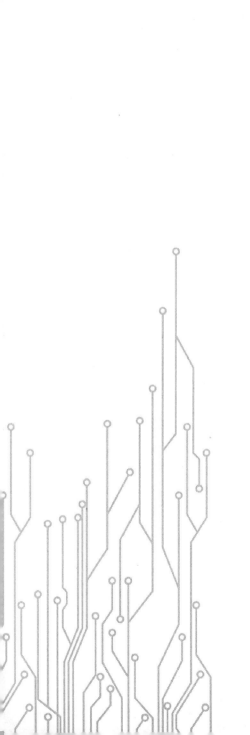

CHAPTER 7

It has been one week since I have officially become a part of the rebel clique. I come back into the apartment, which turns out to be Faustino's, and am greeted as a friend. No longer am I a threat; I have become an ally. Turns out that they need someone who isn't on the radar of The Fisk officials, and I fill that role.

While at this first meeting, I learn a lot that I hadn't known about the city and my new partners themselves.

West and Faustino have apparently been friends for a long time, and neither had wanted to take on the AG lifestyle. I can tell they have some deep personal reason, but they don't share it with Alexis and me. They do tell us the rest of their story: a few weeks before the Shift they made plans to meet up as soon as they awoke. They had already been planning their escape before they even moved to The Fisk. To make sure they weren't shipped off to separate places, Faustino had bribed an official to make sure they would end up in the same generation in the same city. They planned to lay low and not attract attention until they could escape. However, right before the procedure,

West went berserk and had to be sedated. This struggle had put a warning sign on his back even before he got here.

I observe the two guys as they tell their story. West will share a sentence, then Faustino will mention something West forgot. Then the story will continue in the same scattered manner as before. The two have obviously been friends for ages, but they still seem to be a bit wary of Alexis and me. Their body language is more relaxed than when I first met them, but they still tense up when questions pry too deep. West, I have come to learn, is more of a wildcard than Faustino. He is open and funny, but also has a hair-trigger temper that flares at the smallest of things. Yet, he is more colloquial and easier to be around than his friend. I have come to know him as hardworking and good-natured. Faustino, on the other hand, is quite the opposite of West. He is more reserved, and rarely joins in as the rest of us joke and make sarcastic comments about the AG lifestyle. He is all business.

Alexis had been from an entirely different city, but she secretly always hated the idea of living only a fraction of her deserved life in a shell. She doesn't really tell us much else about herself at that first meeting. I have learned, however, that they all came together on the day of the awakening. The two guys had heard Alexis muttering rebellious statements from a bench near where they had prearranged to meet up. The three immediately joined forces. I had stumbled upon them during their first meeting so, lucky for me, I haven't really missed much.

They are all a few years older, with Faustino being the oldest at twenty-five when the Shift occurred. West is twenty-three, and Alexis is nineteen. While at Faustino's, we talk about age for a while. I hadn't realized that these identity chips were designed to last forever, and with new shells consistently available, death is almost impossible. The Fisk and all the other AG cities had been designed that way, to have a fixed population, well, forever. In the handbook we all received, it told us that in an effort to give everyone a clean slate, a new age system was created. In the new system, we would all adopt the same age: one AGY, or one alternation of generation year. It is extremely odd to know that now Catherine-Grace is as old as me, and I am as old as everyone in the city.

West says that he heard that once every one hundred cycles, the populations will be allowed to be shuffled, meaning that if you so desire and have the money to afford it, you could move to another city or change generations. It would be like bathing in the fountain of youth. You could become a new person every one hundred years.

"But what if someone got, you know, tired of living?" I ask at that first meeting.

Alexis replies by explaining that she doesn't think the builders thought that far out; because of the rapid population growth and the lack of time to find a solution, minimal planning had been done. Faustino also points out that life in The Fisk is perfect for maintaining a happy mind. There is work to keep you occupied, free time to have to yourself, and even crazy trips you could take—for large sums of money—that would give you a taste of adventure, not to mention the hundred-year shuffle. People need goals, he points out, and there are certainly many to take. Former teachers and professors can find work as educators, and those who desire could take classes and even enroll in full-time schooling for a semester or longer. All of a sudden, Alexis, who has been thoughtful and quiet, poses a question that stop all of us in our tracks.

"What about children? What happened to all the people who weren't old enough or mature enough to fully function in society?" she asks. Silence filling the room.

"My youngest brother," I suddenly blurt out. "He was only nine at the Shift. What happened to him?" And perhaps even more importantly, *Why have I not wondered this before now?* I add internally. Had I assumed that he had gone to live on his own like the rest of us? As I think about it, I realize that the question of his whereabouts never even crossed my mind. *What does that say about me?* I ask myself as guilt burns through my body.

I had assumed that everyone became their own AG citizen, but suddenly that doesn't make any sense at all. Nine-year-olds couldn't be living all alone! What about the babies who needed a caring mother to protect and nourish them? You can't stick them in twenty-year-old shells. My palms get sweaty and my head spins. How have I not noticed all the answers I have never been given. The looks on the three around me tell me that they had never thought about it either.

We all sit there, staring at each other.

"I have no idea," West finally puts forth with a scared expression, like he doesn't want to find out.

"I bet it isn't good, or we would have heard bragging comments about it in those Shift endorsement commercials," Alexis says with a long face.

We debate asking one of the guards stationed throughout the city. But in the end, we decide it would draw too much unneeded attention, and the answers wouldn't be true or beneficial anyway. It couldn't be good is our consensus, and we come to the resolution that if we ever get out of the city, we would devote our efforts to finding out.

Even though I agree with the decision we make, in the back of my mind is still that nagging question: *What happened to Cane?*

We push forward though. Our drive to escape is strong, but we need a plan. Alexis puts forth that she will start learning about our shells. She wants to find out whether or not they can continue to live without a chip keeping the memories in. If we are going to take off the docks, we probably need to know if we can survive without them. If not, then we would have to think of another plan because all the docks have alarm systems that will activate if they go outside the city without special clearance codes. The docks have to come off. Faustino is chosen to be the one looking for information about the identity chips. He will try to learn everything he can about them, so that, eventually, we can find a way to safely remove both the chip and the dock. As a group, we decide that West will focus on working and earning money for food and whatever else we may need. The officials are probably keeping an eye on him, and there is no reason to have him researching chip removal procedures. He agrees, with some grumbling, that he will lie low and go about as a normal citizen.

"Would we need real bodies?" Alexis asks.

That's when I contribute. Just the day before, when I was out exploring the city, I had seen a flyer for a "body swap." The idea is that if you don't like the way your shell looks, or you want a more individual look, you could pay to have your memories transferred to a new, real body. At the time, it had given me chills. Bodies have become a fashion statement, like a jacket you could change if you decide you don't like it enough. But now, it may be useful. I tell the rest of the group, and we decide that if we are going to need to have real bodies, we are going to need a lot of money to pay for the transfer for all of us. So, my job becomes helping West to earn money. Also, Alexis points out, I need to act as normal as possible. I am the only one of them who hasn't done anything to alert the attention of the city officials.

Our meeting concludes with the decision to hold another in a week at Alexis's apartment. Until then, we would all devote ourselves to the tasks at hand and work at our different assignments.

I throw myself into work. I feel a renewed motivation now that I am working toward a common goal with others, rather than trying to pay for something all on my own. I am working on my millionth gardening project as I try to earn money. Working is actually oddly enjoyable. So far, I have planted trees, watered a park, and even signed up to help organize a concert in a couple of weeks. My small pool of friends, well, acquaintances, is also steadily growing as I branch out and meet more people through work. I catch up with Will one day while attempting to lever a young banana tree into its designated hole. I am having considerable trouble lifting the heavy sapling off the cart while I quietly ridicule my shell for not being stronger.

"Stupid shell, if I am stuck in you for the next forever, you are going to have to do better than this," I say as I try to use my shoulder as a lever. Completely failing, I step away from the cart and the tree, trying to examine it for a weakness. It will not keep me defeated for long.

"Hey, Mira!" says a voice behind me. I turn and see that it is Will.

He jogs over with an easy stride, and I notice for the first time how attractive a shell can be. His shaggy brown hair and strong build make him quite the looker. I let out a happy sigh. Even the bizarrely patterned pants and vest of Fisk style can't detract too much from his tan skin and white smile. A second later, I catch myself and realize exactly how weird those thoughts are.

Ew, ew, ew! Mira, no crushing on fake bodies. That is not allowed.

I shudder, compose myself again, and point at the banana tree. "Hey, Will, do you think you could help me get this tree out of the cart and into that hole? It's mocking me."

"Sure, I saw you struggling, and it would be cruel not to help," he says with a grin. I laugh then flash a pretend offended face. I have to remind myself a second time that shells are weird and certainly not something to be attracted to. He walks over and wraps his arms around the offending tree. With a grunt, he leans back and pulls the tree with him, dropping it in the hole as soon as the base dangles over it.

"That was easy," he says as he casually dusts off his hands, barely holding back a grin.

"That's because your guy shell was made stronger than my wimpy, weak one," I joke.

Will, however, does not seem to appreciate the joke. A frown crosses his formerly jovial face. "Don't say that," he says. "I'm sure your shell is plenty strong." He won't meet my eyes.

"What happened to a joke? I was just messing around," I counter, as a slight irritation pricks me. *What is up with this?*

"I don't think it's cool to joke about your shell. They are a great gift, and we wouldn't be able to have this lifestyle if we didn't have the shells," he says slowly, still avoiding my gaze.

I look at him, dumbfounded. "You know, I am allowed to make jokes about my shell, or anything else I feel like," I say slowly.

"Well, I don't think that's appropriate," Will replies stiffly. "I think I am going to go back over. One of those holes doesn't quite

look like it was dug deeply enough." He turns and half jogs away from me and proceeds to widen the already big enough hole.

I look like a fish as I stand here with my mouth open. He keeps his back to me, and I keep my wide eyes on him. What on earth was that? I was making a joke, poking fun, nothing more. And from what I know about him, Will likes jokes. No one could really be *that* adamant about supporting the shells. *Well that was ridiculous,* I think to myself as I turn back around and proceed to cover the base of the banana tree with dirt.

I never see Will again. Not in a single one of the next hundred projects do I see him.

Even with those hundreds of projects, money still comes very slowly. Food also turns out to be very expensive. But it does make sense—the city couldn't have people getting rich immediately, or it would make life too easy. That knowledge doesn't soothe my anger though; I am having trouble saving up the money for the bodies we may have to buy. After all, I pay for Alexis's and my own meals. West is having similar troubles. I meet up with him on a gardening project one day, and turns out, he isn't making the boatloads of money he hoped for either since he is paying for Faustino's and his own meals.

Before our second meeting arrives, Faustino tells me that I should bring the food for lunch. After making a significant dent in our funds and filling my arms with bags of noodles and dumplings, I ride the elevator to Alexis's room on the second floor. I idly think about the fact that a week ago, I wouldn't have been able to bring food like this anywhere without indulging first. Within a week, dining on the rich delicacies of the city had calmed my appetite for them. I gaze out the glass of the elevator onto the lawn. There are several groups having picnics on the impeccably kept expanses of grass. It looks like so much fun, but I know we couldn't be having our rebellious meetings out there. Oh well, if the insurgent life means no picnic meetings, I suppose I will have to learn to cope.

I pull my gaze away from the lawn and stride confidently down the hall. I am no longer intimidated by the luxury of the apartments or the people in them. I make my way down to Alexis's apartment, shifting my bags to give me a free hand. As soon as I knock, she opens the door and I step in. I am the first one here, but Alexis is practically bursting with news.

"What's up with you? You look like one of my brothers when they've had too much sugar," I tell her as she zips around.

"Well, I've got huge news. When are Faustino and West getting here? I'm about to explode. Oh, this is so huge!" she says, almost faster than I can understand.

"Then tell me already!" I say.

"No, I don't want to explain it twice. Ugh! Are Faustino and West ever going to get here?" Alexis says as she paces around the room.

While Alexis busies herself with wearing holes in the carpet, I open up the food. Elegant curls of steam rise up out of the container. I quickly destroy them as I thrust my chopsticks upon a dumpling. It is my first time ever using the wooden sticks to eat. I quickly give up and resort to a fork.

"I wonder if shell bodies can get fat," I think aloud as I start my second dumpling. I feel somewhat self-conscious being the only one eating. After a moment of deliberation, I conclude it would be kindest to offer some of my exotic banquet to Alexis.

"Alexis, you want any?" I ask while blowing on a bite of noodles, although I don't really intend on sharing my feast.

"No, I actually haven't eaten anything since lunch yesterday."

I think she saw the alarm in my face because she quickly explained herself.

"It has to do with getting our minds and our memories to separate from the chips. You will understand later, I promise," she reassures me, all the while continuing to walk grooves in the floor.

"Should I stop eating then?" I ask while frowning down at my delicious food. My shell has an addiction to Chinese.

"No, you're fine. Keep stuffing your face," she tells me with a smirk.

"I don't know if I would be able to stop if I tried," I inform her, only halfway joking. "Gardening is seriously hard work."

"Hmm hmm," Alexis replies, but I can tell her mind is somewhere else. We fall into peaceful silence, each of us caught up in our own thoughts.

About five minutes later, the guys finally decide to grace us with their presence. We exchange our usual sarcastic greetings, but then sit down to discuss what we have learned. I'm glad we do, because I feel Alexis seriously would explode if we wait any longer. I quickly pass out the food I had brought while my overly energetic friend explains herself.

"So, I was looking through some of the digital books on my touchpad and found one written by Dr. Holly Rushweld, who worked with Richard Calvin to develop the first shells. The book was incredibly long and boring, so I skimmed through most of it, but one of the chapters talked about the benefits of the shell. The first thing mentioned was that the shells had a really strong connection with the chip, since the dock had been installed so early on. The book went on to talk about how human bodies really couldn't compare in terms of physical strength and healing speed.

"That one section got me thinking though. The shells had strong connections with the chip in comparison to human bodies, right? So real bodies must have a weaker connection. Once I connected those dots, I started to research the human connection with the identity chip. Turns out, real bodies partially reject the dock because it is a foreign contraption. There is still enough connection to keep the memories in the body, but it is weak enough to be broken.

"After I learned that, my theory was all but proven. You see, I heard, back before the Shift, about this kid with a rare disease who needed to be transferred to a new body. They would have used a shell, but there weren't any available. So the dad offered to have his memories transferred to a chip so that his kid could use his body until more shells came in. He hadn't wanted his child to have to go into hibernation mode. Luckily, they got the child out of his diseased body in time, and they immediately disposed of it so the illness wouldn't spread.

"However, the hasty procedure to get a dock onto the dad's neck and remove his memories hadn't been done quite right. The link between the dock and neck was therefore very weak, even weaker than the regular human connection, but the doctors didn't know this, and they proceeded to install the child's memories into his dad's body. Everything seemed fine for a short while, but it was quickly discovered the child couldn't digest food. The dock didn't connect to the part of the brain that controlled those functions, and since the connection of a real body to the chip is already pretty weak, the bond was especially fragile. When they tried to remove the child's memories from the body, it didn't work. The child was permanently inside his dad's body.

"The way it was explained to me was that, in a real body, the brain is stronger due to the fact that it has been making memories since birth, unlike the shells, which are grown memory-free. The brain can therefore seize all of the memories and hold them permanently if it believes the dock has become a threat. In this case, the dock was preventing the ability to digest. The child soon regained the ability to eat and digest food once his memories and new brain fully merged, the dock was removed because it was no longer of any use, and his dad got the shell that was meant for the child.

"The point is, we can pull our memories off the chips entirely if we are in human bodies. Then, unfortunately, we would have to starve ourselves until our minds came off the chips, but it could potentially allow us to safely remove the docks and escape the city. I see how you are looking at me, and I know it sounds crazy, but it's the only way I have found that could allow us to safely remove the docks. And it's perfect, because I think my body isn't a shell after all. I can be the one to test it!"

Alexis finishes her long story and sits staring at us expectantly. The three of us reel at all the information she has thrown at us. She seems very excited about starving herself.

"How do you know you aren't in a shell?" Faustino finally asks.

"Well, a couple of reasons," she starts. "First of all, my skin is a little paler than everyone else's, and I have more freckles than I have seen on any of the other shells. Those don't really prove anything, but I think this does. Look, I have a birthmark. How weird is that?"

On her left leg, on the back of her knee, is a darker patch of skin about the size of a quarter. It is kind of shaped like a potato. It is in such a weird spot that I never noticed it before. Wow, she really is in a human body—no shell has those marks. Shell skin has no blemishes like birthmarks, and if one somehow did, it would have been disposed of.

"How long have you been thinking about this?" I ask.

"Well I had the hunch before the Shift, when I first heard that story about the boy with the disease. So I have been monitoring my food intake ever since I got here so I can start right away if I needed to. I haven't done anything drastic yet, but I'm ready if you think it might work. I think I should go all the way and stop eating altogether. This could be our chance to see if we can remove the docks safely. Isn't that what we want?"

I don't know about West and Faustino, but this does not sound like a safe plan, even though it is possible it could work. I don't want to shoot down her idea, though, because she seems so excited about it. It makes sense and must have been why she hadn't eaten on the way to that meeting to "decide what to do with me." But what if doctors had fixed that problem? I'm not sure I am willing to risk it.

"Well—" I start, but West interrupts me.

"I think you should do it. We will raise as much money as we can to get ourselves real bodies, and hopefully, we can break out soon," he says.

It shocks me to hear him say that. West does realize that Alexis is planning to *starve* herself, right? He is being way too impulsive. We need to plan more. What if doctors really had fixed that problem? Alexis could die. I turn to look at Faustino, who is sitting against the wall chewing thoughtfully.

"I don't think it's safe, guys," I put forth. "Faustino?" I ask, looking for an ally.

After a moment, he replies, "Alexis, it was your research to do. If you think it's safe enough and worth it, then go for it. I found medical documents, and I think I can remove the docks safely with a certain few tools I can easily obtain. Mira, I understand your concern, but it's break out or stay here. I choose the first one. Bodies are only going to get more expensive. We need to act soon."

Okay. Who appointed him leader? This is not okay. We are not starving ourselves. Hello? It's dangerous.

"Hey, Mira, it will be okay. You don't have to do it yet. I will go ahead and try it, and if it works, we can all do it. Either way, no one's forcing you. You can always stay here in the city if you want," Alexis says with a pointed glance.

That is a harsh blow, and she knows it. I now have to agree with her. If I don't, I risk losing the favor of Faustino and West, both of whom I need if I ever want to escape.

"Fine, let's do it," I say after a moment's pause. I immediately regret it as soon as the words are out of my mouth although I don't take it back.

"Great!" West says with way too much enthusiasm. "Now we need to focus on earning money. Faustino, you can join our work force now!" he says with false excitement. Faustino shoots him an evil glare but laughs. His chill week of research has come to an end. Soon all three of us are going to be up to our knees in flowers. Back to work we go. Alexis, on the other hand, will be allowed to do whatever she wants, we decide. It is fair enough because she won't be allowed to eat.

"Okay, so let's meet again in a week?" I suggest. We all know what we need to do.

"Sounds good," the three others say in agreement.

"My apartment at noon?" I offer.

"Let's do it," Alexis says. "But make sure you eat ahead of time, guys. I can hardly stand sitting here watching you guys stuff your faces."

We all promise we will then head out. I have another gardening assignment lined up in an hour, so I start in that direction after leaving

Alexis's apartment building. Operation Break Out of The Fisk is officially in action, even though I'm not entirely sure I want to go through with it.

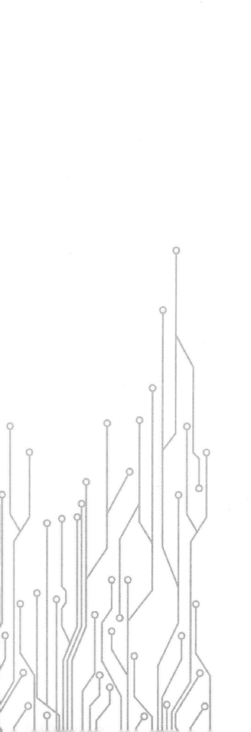

CHAPTER 8

Alexis and I stride through the leafy underside of the clock tower. We are headed out to the lake to hopefully tempt some sun to tan our shells a bit. Because I am continually working outside, I have developed a remarkably severe short sleeve tan line, and I am determined to even it out today. Together, the two of us walk along, linked arm in arm, in the least ridiculous puffy shorts and the plainest tank tops we could find. Alexis has already lost a large amount of weight in her face and it is really beginning to show elsewhere. She starts to truly look like a disturbing walking toothpick. I, in the meantime, am beginning to resemble a marshmallow. I simply have an inability to say no to the rich delicacies of the city.

It is one of the few, and by few, I mean the first, mostly work-free days I have taken. I stretch out my arms, sore from gardening, as we walk along the cobblestone path that leads to the lake. I need a day off. My back is becoming increasingly tight with all the bending and shoveling I have to do. But today, I will relax with the girl I consider my best friend here in The Fisk. We still aren't sisters like

Lilli and I had been, but we are growing closer the more time we spend together.

"You know what's weird?" Alexis asks me after we lie down on the grass beside the calm waters.

"I know what's annoying," I say. "That Faustino and West refused to let us buy towels! I mean, how expensive can two towels possibly be?" I eye the sketchy grass. It is likely infested with flesh-eating ants.

"Well, I suppose I agree," she says thoughtfully.

"With me?" I ask hopefully.

"No," she replies with a laugh. "With them. Wasting money on towels seems like a pretty silly thing to do."

"Hmph, whatever. So what's weird?" I ask.

"What's weird is that someone else, actually nine someone else's, have lived in this same body before me. Like, our shells or bodies or whatever are used. Isn't that bizarre?" Alexis says as she sprawls on her back, splaying out her arms and legs.

I stop eyeing the grass and bring my hand up to my face. "Yeah, that is weird—like nine other people have chewed on these nails, although it has always been this same mouth."

"That's *exactly* what I was thinking, Mira," Alexis says as she sarcastically smiles and rolls her eyes at me. "But really, in generation one, my shellmate might have broken my arm, and I would never know about it."

"What's so odd about that though?" I ask.

"I feel like I have this whole secret history, and I want to know what it is. Even outside of what has happened to my shell, what happened in the other generations? Did they have people trying to escape?" Alexis queries as she closely examines the palm of her hand, as though it will give her answers.

"Alexis, don't say it so quietly; yell it for the whole city to hear. Or at least loud enough for that official *right over there* to hear that we are trying to escape," I say with a pointed glance at the official striding along the path beside the lake. Luckily, he is walking away from us and is clearly out of earshot.

"Right, right, that was a stupid thing to say out loud, but it's interesting isn't it? What kind of secrets does The Fisk hold?"

"Yeah, like what happens to those who get caught? Do the officials let them wake back up and keep causing havoc in their second year? Or will their chips somehow 'get lost' in the system?" I muse.

"Exactly what I was wondering," Alexis replies.

We fall into a thoughtful silence for the next several hours as the sun browns our skin. We only occasionally speak, reminding each other to flip over when we spend too long lying on one side.

We part ways after leaving the lake, and I head off to complete yet another gardening assignment, while Alexis goes back to her apartment. We will meet up again after I finish working. First, however, I am intent on getting a good meal. I watch her as we walk off, no lunch for her. I have to say though, she takes the not-eating task incredibly well, much better than I would have anyway.

I am incredibly itchy from the grass, but my tan has evened out enough that I am satisfied. It was worth it, but now I wish I had some cream to put on my itchy arms and legs. I know West, and especially Faustino, would immediately veto my idea. They are seriously intent on spending no more than we absolutely have to. I can still take pleasure in a delicious meal though, and there is nothing they can do about it.

Heh heh, I'm such a rebel.

For lunch, I decide on a little street cart called Around the Circumference. It has a pretty cool story behind it. The woman who started it is named Isabella Guardez, and she owned a restaurant by the same name before the Shift. Claiming that cooking is in her blood, she walked into City Hall one day and proclaimed that she wanted to open up her restaurant here in The Fisk. They refused to give her a restaurant, but offered her the chance to open up a street cart. She immediately snatched up the offer, and the following day she was wheeling the cart around, open for business. Now there are several different food carts rolling through the city, but hers remains the best.

I purchase some of her Cuban stew and enjoy it thoroughly.

By the time I make it back around to Alexis's, the sun has begun to set. Shadows stretch out behind the buildings, and I walk in and out of the light. Pre-Shift, I would never have been allowed to go out walking this late. I would be tucked safely, or at least relatively safely, back in my apartment with the rest of my family.

The cooling air blowing through The Fisk feels good, and the smell of flowers fills the air. I walk across a bridge over a trickling creek and almost fall off when a loud bullfrog chooses to make its presence known. I know the bounty of life here will never cease to amaze me. I wonder about how life outside the walls will be. If all these plants and creatures live and grow here in the city, I can't imagine what the wildlife outside the cities will look like—it will be like nothing I have ever seen.

Part of me fears being free of the safety of the city. Anything can happen out there. I know, however, that this place is too good to be true. Hardship is a part of life, and that's not to say that life cannot be good. But living forever in an idyllic city full of happy people can't truly be possible. Truth is out there, and freedom is the first step to finding it.

I cross over into Lincolnton Complex, which is where Alexis's apartment is. I head toward the second building from the left. It was brick and stone with impeccably manicured lawns. I walk into the lobby area and look for an elevator. I finally see the golden-doored elevator tucked away in a corner.

I go up to Alexis's apartment, 2G, and knock on the door. She knows I am coming over and opens the door almost immediately. The color scheme of her room is much different than mine, which still sports the rainbow of colors I chose on the first day. Alexis's room, finally changed from the stark whites, is a mix of greens and yellows and blues. It reminds me of the outdoors.

"So how did the job go?" Alexis asks me as I walk in.

"It was good, but boring. I'm getting pretty sick of planting trees in every corner of the city," I complain as I flop down on her bed.

"Hey, it hopefully won't last much longer, and then all your work will have paid off," Alexis says.

"Yeah, I know. Speaking of which, what exactly are we planning to do if we do break out?" I ask. It has been bugging me for a while, not knowing exactly what I am heading for. In our meetings, they all seem to know more. They look so sure about what we are doing, while I am left asking all the questions. I have the feeling the three of them are talking without me. *Not cool, guys.*

"I don't even know exactly," Alexis says while running her fingers through her hair. "I think the loose plan that Faustino put together involves going to one of the old cities from the past for supplies and stuff, maybe camp out there for a while. After that, I'm honestly not sure."

"Do you even think Faustino knows what he is doing?" I ask, sneakily looking over to see how she reacts. Faustino has been steadily getting on my nerves more and more lately, especially in regards to money. He acts like he is completely in charge all the time. I understand that he is the one who came up with the idea to leave in the first place. Yet, it almost seems like he is micromanaging the rest of us so as to draw our attention away from his cobbled-together plans.

Alexis doesn't seem fazed by my question. She answers thoughtfully. "I don't think he quite understands exactly what is going on. He seems to be the type that is used to understanding what is happening and being in control. I trust him though. He isn't going to let us follow through on a poorly put together plan."

"Yeah, that makes sense," I say, trying not to let a frown cross my face. Alexis clearly talks with the guys, or at least Faustino, a lot more than I do.

Alexis suddenly laughs.

"You know what I've been wondering lately?" she asks.

"No?"

"If Faustino cares that his shell is white," Alexis says, with a thoughtful look on her face.

"I had that same thought," I tell her. "I thought his name might mean that he is Hispanic, but I suppose it really doesn't mean anything."

"That's true," she replies, "but what if he was? Think how awful that would be for him. He would have lost so much of his cultural identity."

"I don't know. I suppose he would have to deal with it," I reply. What a weird idea. If all my life I had been another ethnicity, how would I feel if I were forced to be white like everyone else? The more I think about it, the more likely it seems that that is part of the reason Faustino hates the system. It has taken his entire culture out in one swift blow.

"Do you think they can make shells of other ethnicities?" Alexis asks.

"Hmm, I want to say that they probably can. We have such crazy technology that I can't imagine them not being able to make them."

Alexis nods her head in agreement.

"But," I continue, "making a whole new kind of shell would have to cost an insane amount of money, and it's likely that it's easier to use the shells we already have."

"Yeah, but think of how much diversity that takes away. So much identity is stripped away in forcing everyone to look the same," Alexis says sadly.

"Of course, they would never think to tell us anything like that. They sold it like we would all be equal, but they were stripping us of the differences that helped to define us as individuals," I say. When I am around Alexis or West and Faustino, it becomes so much easier to remember why I hate The Fisk. When I am alone, the perfection of everything around me seems to brainwash me, distracts me from what hides beneath the surface.

Alexis and I talk late into the night until we are yawning and barely carrying the conversation. I trudge back across the city under the stars, dreading my next assignment in the morning. The people around me are still wide-awake. Shopping, dining, and living without a care in the world. Those lucky ducks don't have to worry about saving money. I finally make it back to my apartment and sprawl out over my bed without even taking off my ridiculous clothing.

Just before falling asleep, I cross my fingers that we will be able to escape the city soon.

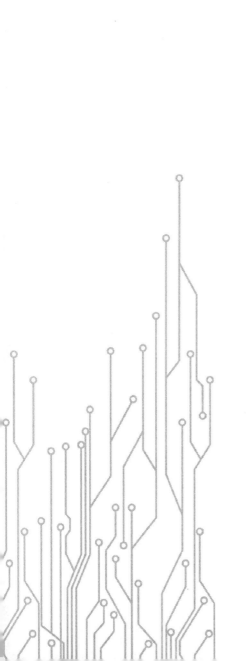

CHAPTER 9

Work is becoming routine for me. I garden, plan, and organize every day, all day long. I learn the ins and outs of different jobs. For example, gardening doesn't pay much unless you design your own project and get it approved. Event coordination doesn't really have a high rate either unless you are the one to design and start the project. The most efficient way to earn money that I have found is to sign up to deliver mail. Someone in the city had decided to start a mail delivery system, The Fisk Express. It is a total hit. People think it is cool and fun to send letters the old-fashioned way. Even though it is not as practical as using digital services, it is more fun. The trend had become widely popular, and the mail delivery system has grown rapidly. I signed up to deliver mail once a week at first. But as I continued in that position, I realized I could earn significantly more than any other job.

Each letter delivered on time counts toward your pay, which is purely productivity based. I soon realize that I can deliver about fifteen to twenty letters an hour, and I can earn double what I get for an hour of gardening. There is a lot of walking to do, though, because the letters are only categorized by whether the apartment destination is on the Royal Oaks Complex or the Lincolnton Complex. It is good that they do that, since the two are on opposite ends of the city, but dashing back and forth between the buildings even in the same complex is tiring. Still, if I am efficient, I can earn a large sum each day.

I bring up investing in a bicycle at one of our weekly meetings, but my idea is shot down. Faustino and West think that a bike would be too expensive and not worth our money. At the time, I think of blurting out how it is actually *my* money so I can do whatever I want with it, but I keep my mouth shut. It isn't worth it to disturb the peace when we are getting so close to our goal.

We are a month and a week into our year of life here in The Fisk. Time is racing by. We know we will need to escape this year because bodies will only become rarer and more expensive. As a group, we have enough money at this point to purchase one body, and we are more than halfway to having enough for a second. Our official plan at the moment is, assuming the whole starving yourself thing works, to start out by getting real bodies. After we are in them, we plan to fast until we can separate our minds from the chips. Then we will remove them and sneak out of the city.

West has done some research on the actual city, and he found that we can get over the wall at pretty much any point we want. The city's security system keeps tabs on its inhabitants through the docks on their necks. The docks apparently do more than put memories into host bodies; they also have a locating system. Along with this locating system is a sort of electric fence mechanism. If the body tries to leave the city without the special coding that allows people to takes trips and such, it will be put into forced hibernation mode until an official reactivates it. So if we could manage to get the docks off—without killing ourselves in the process—we would be practically free.

But the fasting is getting dangerous. Alexis shouldn't be risking it. I have to try to help her. While West, Faustino, and I have been working, Alexis has been losing tons of weight to the point where I am really worried about her. She has been eating and drinking almost nothing and now looks sickly and weak. After that first week, we decide to start holding all our meetings in her apartment so she won't have to go out into the city. Her body is nothing but a bag of bones. We don't want the officials to see and get suspicious, but at the same time, she needs help, and I am determined to get her to stop.

I am heading over to her apartment to try to talk her out of the fast. *Well here goes nothing,* I tell myself as I near my destination. I walk up the stairs to Alexis's apartment building and navigate my way to her room. Despite all my best attempts, I still can't ignore the beauty of the architecture and interior design. None of the apartment buildings have a hotel feel to them; each one has different flairs and accents that make them into a homey place. Alexis's home is no different. The color scheme of her building includes pale yellow tones offset by deep cranberry. There are lounges on the bottom floor where lots of people congregate to catch up over coffee. Halls are wide and well lit with beautiful lamps between each door.

As I near Alexis's room, I prep myself for the conversation I am about to have. I hadn't wanted to bring it up at one of our meetings because I know Faustino and West would disapprove. I am going to try to convince Alexis to stop her fast or, if I can't do that, at least eat something. I brought with me some simple chicken soup and crackers. Her fast has been going on for a month, and she still hasn't been able to fully separate her mind from the chip. She says she could feel that part of her mind moved in completely and that she needs to wait on the rest. I doubt her though. Week after week, the little green light on her dock indicates that her memories are still linked to the chip. She is so blinded by hope and desperation to leave that she only tells herself that it is working. I don't want to say this though. I don't want to crush all her hope. Over those few weeks, she and I have grown really close, and I don't want to lose my closest, well, only friend. West and Faustino are more of partners in crime.

Before she had become so obviously malnourished, we actually used to do stuff together. When I wasn't working or sleeping, we hung out. Most of the time we walked around in the parks and hung out by the lake because everything else cost money, but we always had fun. I also learned a lot about her. I already knew she came from a different city than West and Faustino, but I learned a lot more as time went on.

One of the first secrets she revealed was that she was an orphan. It was a really sensitive topic to her, I could tell. She told me that she had been an orphan since birth, and with the massive population, living life alone had been hard. Alexis grew up in a complex with about two thousand other kids. It was a government facility, and she confided in me that, even with all those kids, she had always felt lonely. Other children found friends and formed close bonds, but she was always on the outside.

When she finally became old enough to leave the facility, she started work at a junky grocery store. At the time, she had been living in a one-room basement apartment in the building neighboring the store. Her six months there were hard, especially since she was so young. There were thousands of unemployed, eligible adults vying for those same higher paying jobs she wanted, so of course she never got them.

Her life turned around when she met Niall. He was in the same situation. His parents had died, and now he was out on his own. He and Alexis became friends and, later, more than friends. Together they worked to build a better life. Apartments became cheaper as people flocked to AG cities, and life became easier and simpler. They moved to a better apartment and got better jobs. They even talked about getting married. Life was still hard, but amazing at the same time. When describing it to me Alexis had said, "It was like a tarnished golden locket. Underneath all the hardship was a beautiful life that I truly loved."

They had only known each other for a year and a half when the Shift came. Like my family and me, tearful good-byes were said, then they were separated forever. Alexis said she knew for a fact that they were shipped to different cities.

"I wouldn't even hate the Shift, or this lifestyle, if it hadn't taken what I had. If I had been a hobo on the streets, I would have loved it. Although my life was difficult, it wasn't hollow. What I had was love and a future before me that I built myself. I worked two jobs to help pay for that new apartment. Niall had done the same. When, suddenly, all our hard work was thoughtlessly cast aside to make room for whatever fake substitute this is," Alexis had poured out as she gestured at the world around her.

I sympathize completely. She knows exactly what it is like to have your plans shredded before your eyes. In fact, she knows it better than I do. That's why it is going to be so hard to convince her to stop the fast. She wants out so badly. Her one desire is to start over and work for her life herself. She never directly says it, but I think she feels she doesn't deserve what has been given to her. Her whole life she was raised to work hard to earn what she wants. In her mind, it is probably too good to be real. So I have to do this right. I need Alexis to eat something. I care about her so much, and it kills me to see her killing herself. I finally reach her door, and I reach up to knock. My fist falters for a second. Should I really do this? After a moment's hesitation, I hide the food I brought behind another doorway a few rooms down. It will be too obvious that I want her to eat, and she may jump to the wrong conclusions. With my soup barely visible, I rap my fist on the door.

Tap. Tap.

"Hold on," I hear Alexis say feebly from the other side of the door.

She sounds awful. Her voice soft, barely there, and judging by the time it took for her to reach the door, she can't be in peak physical condition either. My poor friend is dying. It is time to help. She opens the door and I step through. I glance down at her wrist. The bone is clearly defined and her hand shakes as she takes it off the knob.

"Hey, Alexis," I say softly. I fear that if I speak too loudly she will shatter to pieces. She looks so fragile. Her movements are slow and shaky. The moment she reaches her bed, she collapses down upon it. I go and sit down on the foot of the bed beside her since there are no other chairs in the room. After all, we are saving up for real bodies. New furniture is a luxury that we can't afford.

How do I go about this? I think. I can't come right out and say that I don't believe her plan is working. Doing that will make her defensive. I have to be careful, but on the other hand, kissing up to her isn't going to work either. We had become really close friends, but there is still a certain tension between us. I am the kid who barged in on a meeting and shoved myself upon them and their scheme to escape the city. In a way, I am still on the outside. Alexis might think I am conspiring against her, Faustino, and West if I don't present my argument right.

"Well, are you just going to sit there?" Alexis asks while smiling broadly. She is poking fun at me, but seeing that she is happy and still hopeful makes my job even harder.

"You caught me; I planned on not moving until you became a pile of bones. Judging by the look of you it should only be a few minutes though," I say. I try to make my answer as lighthearted as possible, but a hint of my seriousness comes through. She really does look like she is about to die. Alexis's body is pale, shrunken, and exhausted, even sickening to look at.

"Oh, don't be stupid, Mira, I'm about to be free of this horrible dock forever, and you are going to ruin it." She is still joking around, but I guess she hears what I am hinting at, because her voice carries seriousness.

"Your voice sounds like it belongs to my great-grandmother. No wait, my great grandmother's dying cat—you seriously sound awful." It is time to get to the point.

"Leave it be, Mira, I'm getting you out of this city by fasting. Besides, I have eaten a few crackers and those nasty pills that West got me. I'm clearly still alive." The conversation is barreling down the tracks, out of control, but I have never been one to shy away.

"But don't you feel like it's never going to happen? You have been going at this for a long time, but the signal on your dock still says your memories are linked to the chip. Do you *really* still think it's going to work?" All the lighthearted fun leaves my voice when I reach that last sentence, and the way I say it kind of implies that it is hopeless. It really looks like it is. Alexis is dying. West and Faustino support it. Neither guy takes any hint that perhaps this isn't going to work. At this point, Alexis is starving herself for an empty cause, and, in the end, she would die. No leaving the city then. Our research is from older books. Surely old problems would have been solved by now.

Alexis icily stares at me, as though she can read my thoughts. She finally says, with a haunting look in her eyes, "I will die, or I will leave this city. If you aren't willing to do the same thing then I question whether or not you are with us."

Wow. That escalated quickly. It went from banter to cold calculation in less than a minute. I must hold the record for worst confrontation skills. Ever. Time to attempt to clean this up before the bag of bones named Alexis freaks out on me. I bet the starvation is affecting her brain.

"You know that I'm with you one hundred and ten percent. If you die, we lose our biggest asset—someone in a real human body. If we are going to get out of here, we are going to need you. If you're dead, you aren't helping us. Not to mention the fact that if someone dies, they are going to investigate it. We would be found out, and who knows what they would do with us. Give us shorter lives? Make us live each one of the cycles? That would be the worst, to never stop living. No matter what you want, Alexis, you definitely won't be doing us a favor by killing yourself. In fact, it wouldn't be fair to allow yourself to die and sentence the rest of us to stay here, forever stuck in the alternation of generation cycle," I say with an edge to my words. I know I am being logical, but I hate how it sounds like I am threatening her. I want to protect her as a friend, but I know it is coming across harshly.

"Not to mention that I would lose one of the only friends I have," I say, trying to take the sting off of what I said before. It really doesn't feel right. I want to help her, but the feeling is growing inside me that she doesn't care about me as much as I thought.

"Your argument is stupid. You know as well as I that you could simply buy a human body and do the experiment yourself. Besides, I'm sure there are bunches of people out there in the city that we don't know who would love to take my place. I have nothing to lose. Fake life or no life, they are basically the same to me. But on the chance that this does work, that I do get the dock off and get free from the city, it would all be worth it. I would be free to live the remainder of my years working on things I actually cared about and providing for myself. I want that, Mira. To be proud of what I've worked hard for and not have it handed to me on a plate; it's what I crave. You might think it's prideful, but I don't care. I can feel my mind separating from the chip, piece by piece. I'm almost there. Stop trying to take this from me." She shoots a glare at me then turns away to lie down, turning her face from me.

You don't have anything to lose? What about our friendship? She makes it seem like that isn't even a factor in her decision. She totally ignores my comment about me missing her. That digs deep. It means that my grand total of real friends in The Fisk is back down to zero.

"What about me? I would miss you," I say, trying to ignore the stinging behind my eyes. There is no way I will let her skirt the question.

"I want to get out of here, at any cost." She doesn't even look at me when she says that, only curls up tighter on her bed, still facing away. She doesn't understand. She doesn't care. I am wrong about her. She doesn't care about me; she doesn't care about anything but leaving. The shock rolls over me.

"Then maybe I should look at it that way too!" I yell, furious and hurt that I have been so misguided.

Alexis says nothing; she doesn't even move. The only sound I hear is a sigh leaving her lips. She doesn't even care enough to apologize. Well then, I angrily rationalize, I should forget about what she wants and do what's best for me, and I know that my life will be over if she dies. There is no way I would ever have enough freedom to research and find another way out of the city if the city officials already suspected that I played a part in Alexis's death. It is clear now that she no longer cares about me, and that I am on my own. Faustino and West would support Alexis and I would be stuck in the city. Alexis would undoubtedly tell the guys that I have turned against them. There is no way I wouldn't be kicked out of the group. West has a short temper, and Faustino believes in our plan too much to give up now. I don't think either of them has the big picture in mind. If Alexis dies, life is over for all of us.

Trying to find a new alliance would be too risky. I had gotten lucky stumbling upon my three current partners, and I can't risk losing them. At the same time, Alexis remains my closest friend in the city, despite everything that has happened. I don't want her to die, but it looks like I have to do something before she ceases to do anything. Her death would be my own. I can't let her die because I will never be able to escape then. But if I do nothing, I will lose the support of the only people I know who could help me escape. It is a lose-lose situation. Ten minutes before, I had been purely focused on helping my friend, but now that I discover how one sided our friendship is, I have turned to protecting myself and my mission to escape.

My anger fuels me as I decide that it is time to take my life into my own hands. Alexis doesn't care about me, so it is time to shove aside my friendship with her and think about myself. I connect the dots and realize that she can't convince Faustino and West that I am going rogue if she isn't around. I need Faustino and West to get out of the city, but not Alexis. It's not like I can hide her though. Then she could still die. No, hiding her away is not the answer. I should turn her in. Then she will be out of the way and will be nursed for her malnutrition. The time it would take until the doctors could get her back to full health would hopefully be long enough to find another way to escape The Fisk. By that time, West, Faustino, and I would be long gone. The question is would she betray me before I get the chance to leave?

I try to think like Alexis. If I were stabbed in the back, I would be trying my best to get the knife into the offender's back. But what if everyone was watching me? What if the knife was a secret I shouldn't have? I couldn't make myself out to look like a killer or risk longer or permanent containment. Then they would take away my knife. Revenge would have to wait until after I was released. I pull my thoughts back to myself and examine my reasoning. If I turn Alexis in for medical attention, with no mention of the whole rebel thing, she wouldn't be able to use that information against me without revealing herself as well. She could lie, I suppose, but eventually the trail would lead back to her.

The plan is golden—evil, but also golden. I am, after all, most likely saving her life. It might not be the life she wants but tough luck, sometimes that's what you get. My stomach twinges at the thought of what I am going to do, but she doesn't care about my future anymore. The least I can do is return the favor.

CHAPTER 10

I need to act now. Faustino and West have been running mail all afternoon and have a gardening project to oversee on the other side of town. We all tend to come hang with Alexis in her apartment when we have free time, but hopefully their jobs would keep them busy. It is about ten minutes until their project starts, but since they organize the project, they would be getting there early to supervise.

While I have been scheming, little miss bony menace has fallen asleep, although she may have been faking to get rid of me. I plan to turn her in as soon as I leave so she won't have time to betray me to the guys, but I walk over and give her my parting words.

"I'll miss you, but I am doing it because I love you." I am about to change her future with a few simple words.

I quickly and quietly leave her room. On the way out, I trash the food I brought. The wasted money makes me mad, but I don't plan on eating it. Soup is not my thing, and I have plenty of money to buy better food. In fact, I have enough money to pay for a new body all by myself. I guess my work ethic had paid off after all. I wonder if I even need Faustino and West. Best not get rid of them too soon though. Never waste a valuable resource. Faustino is probably the more useful of the two, because he is the only one who has figured out how to safely remove the docks. I would rid myself of West, but, unfortunately, the genius and the hothead come as a package deal.

This new position of power has quickly gone to my head. I need to cool it. I also have to figure out what I am going to tell Faustino and West. Probably something along the lines of a guard came to check up on her because they noticed through the GPS in the dock that she hadn't left her room in a while. It is believable enough to fool the both of them. I will worry about that later though—right now, it is time to get my best friend put in custody. *Wow, I sound like such a nice person. Oh well, better hurry.*

I step outside the apartment building and breathe in the fresh air, one of the perks of an AG city—not a reason to stay, of course. I scan my surroundings for one of the familiar city officials out on duty. They really are rather nice. I had once asked one where I could attach a hose so that I could water some freshly planted grape vines, and he had been very helpful.

After walking around for a moment, I spot one casually leaning against a light post. I prep myself and channel a worried best friend character, which really isn't too hard since that's who I already am. The worried part has to be amped up a bit. I put a slightly frantic look on my face and rush over to the officer, who hasn't seen me yet.

"Excuse me, sir; I think my friend is really sick. She isn't eating and she just lies around in her room all day and refuses to come out or eat anything. My friends and I have visited and tried to talk to her but she won't listen. I'm so worried about her, she told me not to do anything about it, but I couldn't help myself. I think she might be . . . dying." I spit out my story as fast as I can, hoping that my words sound nervous and panicked. However, I pause as I say that last part to add emphasis that I am an innocent friend who is terrified of a friend's death.

The guard takes a moment to take in all the information I have given him. After he seems to wrap his head around it, he fixes a professional look on his face and says, "She sounds like she needs serious help." I nod, and he continues, "All right, so what is her name, and where is her apartment? We need to attend to this as quickly as possible. You lead me to where she is, and I will call some medics. Is she really in as bad of a shape as you say?"

"Yes," I say with as much heartfelt emotion as possible, "I'm scared for her!" After pretending to take a shaky breath, I continue to answer the rest of his questions. "Her name is Alexis, and she is up in that apartment building, in apartment 2G," I say while pointing at Alexis's building.

After he identifies himself as Officer White and asks my name, I lead him to Alexis's apartment. With each step forward, I become more nervous. I know my acting has been all right, but Alexis is probably not in peak mental state right now. She might forget to be cautious and somehow reveal that we have been trying to break out, which would pull me into deep trouble.

In. Out. In. Out.

Breathing isn't really helping me, I realize when I start to practically hyperventilate. Luckily, Officer White must have assumed I am scared about Alexis's health and suggests that I should stay outside in the hall while he goes inside to get her. Little does he know that I am turning her over to the people she hates most, but I suppose that staying in the hall would be smart anyway. I should have thought of that. If she can't see me, she will be less likely to jump to conclusions. The Officer knocks on the door while announcing that he is with the police force of The Fisk. There is no noise within the room. Again, Officer White knocks and says that either he will be let in or use his authority to unlock and enter her room anyway. Still no reply.

"Are you sure she is in there, Mira?"

"Positive, I'm not sure why she isn't answering though." It seems odd that Alexis wouldn't open the door for the officer. I mean,

I know that she hates everything about The Fisk, but refusing to let the man in will only get her in deeper trouble.

Officer White turns his attention to the fingerprint scanner that unlocks the door. Only the person living in the apartment and city officials can unlock the door using their prints. He presses his thumb to the scanner, and we hear a click from the lock. He pushes open the door and walk in. Despite wanting to stay in the hall, I find myself heading into Alexis's room. She is lying on her bed, sleeping. It almost makes me laugh. Then I am serious again. I am betraying a friend for her own good, but I still feel guilty. When Officer White sees Alexis, his face pales. He actually looks like he might throw up. She really does look awful. Her skin sags and has lost color since she spends all her time indoors. Her bones are clearly seen poking through the practically translucent sheet of her skin. Then she starts to stir. She rolls over onto her side and faces us as she rubs her eyes. When she finally opens them, they find me and then go to Officer White. Then back to me, then him, and then once again back to me. Her look of surprise is immediately replaced by anger and understanding of what I have done. I should have stayed in the hall. She opens her mouth, but before she can say anything, I rush over and hug her. Hopefully, it will surprise her enough to keep her quiet while I explain. It works. My back toward the officer, I whisper into her ear, "He doesn't know about our plan, just that you are sick."

I pull back out of the hug and she looks at me with contempt. But also, accompanying her contempt is respect for what I have done. I am surprised. I know she would have done the same thing if it meant her chances of escaping the city would have been better, but I had figured her starved brain wouldn't be able to think that clearly.

I clear my voice to make an official apology that will hopefully convince Officer White that I am purely a concerned friend. "Alexis, I am so, so sorry. I know that you didn't want anyone to know that you have an eating disorder. I know how hard it has been for you, and the Shift made it worse. You have to understand that I only wanted to help you." There, that gives Alexis an alibi that won't get me in trouble.

Officer White comes up behind me and pats me on the back. "You did the right thing," he says. "Alexis, you are going to have to come with me. We need to get some food in you. Now." Officer White goes into all-business mode.

Alexis is staring daggers at me. All respect for my little stunt is gone. The officer picks her up as though she were a child and gently starts to carry her toward the door. Suddenly, a cruel smile flickers across her face, but Officer White doesn't see it. Then she turns to him and, like a scared little kid, says, "Thank you so much. I wasn't sure what I should do, and I couldn't get myself to eat anything. I'm so sorry it came to this. I know that you will help me get back to good condition—but wait!" she says as though a thought suddenly occurs to her. Officer White stops in his tracks in confusion. "Would it be all right if I sent a quick message to some friends before we have to go? They will be wondering where I am. I don't want them to get scared." She reaches toward the touchpad on the wall, although she can't quite reach it.

I should have seen this coming. Alexis is going to tell West and Faustino what I have done. This is not okay.

"I'll tell them for you, Alexis," I say as nicely as I can, trying to keep the nervousness out of my voice. "I'm sure they wouldn't want to find out through a message on their touchpads; it would be better if I told them, really."

"We need to get food in you now; you are going to have to use a touchpad at the hospital," Officer White says as he picks up his pace and starts carrying Alexis down the hall.

"Oh, thank you," Alexis pours out.

"I'll get you," she mouths to me as she is carried down the hall. She shoots me a smirk from elevator. She knows she has won.

Just as the elevator doors are starting to close, I see Alexis start coughing. The coughs rack her feeble body, and, in the moment before the doors fully shut, I see her go limp. Has she passed out? What happened? I need to know. Despite the fact that I have traded our friendship for my freedom, I don't want her to die. If she does, then it will be on my conscience forever. Then a thought crosses through my mind: at least if she were dead, she couldn't tell West and Faustino what had happened. *Wait, that's not right. I shouldn't be thinking like this. I'm not that evil. Right?* Well, whether I am evil to the core or not, I need to make sure she is at least still breathing. If she isn't, well, I wouldn't be able to live with myself.

I dart down the stairs; elevators are too slow. I make it out the doors of the building moments after Alexis and Officer White. She isn't moving, but I can see her chest faintly rising and falling with each breath. *Whew, she is alive—only passed out.* Relief floods through me. I have no worries about her once she gets into the emergency vehicle. Once under their care, it will be practically impossible for her to die. If her body becomes too debilitated and they can't fix it, they will probably remove her memories and stick them in a new shell. They probably have some insane technology we are not even aware of here in The Fisk. We are definitely living fifty to a hundred years before our time. All the crazy innovation is in the docks in our necks or behind the scenes. Letting the people work and not having machines do it, gives them a purpose. The people who designed this city are smart, but they hadn't accounted for escapees. Either way, Alexis is in good hands, well, at least safe hands.

I watch Alexis being carted off and then turn to head to my apartment. My dearly departed could still contact West and Faustino and tell them what happened, but I know what to do.

CHAPTER 11

I make it back to my apartment and waste no time in pulling my touchpad out of its dock on the wall. I sprawl out on my bed, which still reflects a bright orange and yellow pattern from when I first mixed up all the colors, and open messaging.

> **To: WEST; FAUSTINO**
> Guys, big, big news. It's about Alexis; she got taken away by an Official.
> We need to talk. Meeting tonight at seven, my place.
> And bring your touchpads.

And, send. They will get the notice after they finish working, which will probably be around six thirty. They won't have eaten dinner yet, most likely, so I figure I will get them food. I need to make sure they believe me one hundred and ten percent, or I am stuck gardening for the rest of my life. My mother always said, "The way to a man's heart is through his stomach." If food is going to help them be more chill and less wary when I tell them what happened to Alexis, then heck yeah I am buying dinner. I'm not above a little buttering up; after all, I sold out my best friend. This is nothing. If worse comes to worst, I can threaten to pull my money from their funds. Ah, there are the threats again, but, whatever, it's not like they could hurt me. A twinge of guilt pricks me in the stomach. I push it aside. I don't need to be distracted by my conscience. I head out to a favorite deli and purchase a platter of sandwiches. It is do or die at this point. As Alexis says, "Fake life or no life, they are basically the same to me." Exactly, and I'm not accepting either one.

As soon as the meeting starts, I plan to tell them what happened to our former partner. My story goes like this: I was talking with Alexis in her apartment when suddenly a red light on her dock started blinking. Then she passed out, and a few minutes later an official came running in. Apparently, the docks have a fail-safe mechanism that alerts authorities when a shell or body is about to die. The officer who came in took her away and shipped her off in an ambulance. Before the car left, though, I heard one of the medical people say she was going to be in rehab for at least the rest of the year because of the trauma of her body shutting down while she was still awake.

I try to keep my story as close to the truth as I can. It will make it easier to act normal. After all, she did pass out. The only difference is I had gone to the official instead of him coming to me. Hopefully, with full stomachs and some good acting on my part, they won't think about it too much. I am banking on the hope that they will be more interested in finding a new way out rather than investigating the sudden disappearance of their friend and partner. Then the plan is to convince them to lend me their touchpads for the night. I will tell them that I need to research other ways to leave the city and having multiple resources open at once would help me find something faster. They will be so dazed from losing Alexis that they won't mind. I will then block Alexis's messages from coming through on their touchpads so she won't be able to tell them what happened. As long as she doesn't send a message within the next three hours, I will be fine.

I sure hope this works.

The guys arrive almost exactly at seven. They are tired and worn looking. Their shirts are still dirty from gardening, and West is sopping wet. They trudge in, and I try to lighten the heavy mood by bringing up a funny story.

"What happened to you?" I ask him as he stands there soaking my carpet.

"Oh, you mean my new haircut?" West asks with a knowing smile. None of us really have any time or extra money to spend on personal maintenance, but West needs it. His hair is getting ridiculously long, almost shoulder length. He knows what I was asking about though. He is acting dumb.

"Oh yeah, that's what I meant. Your mop of hair is looking quite moppy today, West. But seriously, what happened to the rest of you? Did you try to take a shower with one of the hoses? Everyone knows you need it," I reply.

"Some girl named Calyx was having trouble with one of the hoses and propped it up on a bench facing me when she discovered a kink in the line. She unbent it, and I experienced an unexpected rainstorm." I laugh out loud. Even though this is going to be a somber meeting, I can't help it. "Oh, you think that's funny, Mira?" he asks me, his tone hinting at retaliation. "Well, ya know, I'm reeeeaaaallllyyy tired after all that gardening. I'm going to lie down here on this convenient bed."

I try to stop him but I can't reach him in time. He lays himself out over my entire bed. "This is soooooo not funny!" I try to say, but I can't help but laugh at his antics. West starts making sheet angels on my bed.

While we joke around, Faustino finds the food. He pops open the container, and we all head over to stuff our faces with sandwiches of all varieties.

"How much did this cost?" Faustino asks while chewing thoughtfully. He is still the most serious and thoughtful of our group.

"Not as much as you would think," I answer. I have been careful to always keep my balance high enough to afford a body at any time, but I have been treating myself to progressively better and more expensive meals as I earn even more.

We eat and sit for a moment in silence until West brings up the topic of Alexis. Both guys look over at me expectantly. It is time to pull out my acting skills. I clear my throat and tell them what I rehearsed earlier. It almost upsets me how easily the lies come, but I put it into my character. A few minutes later, I finish, and silence once again sweeps over the room.

"So, she really is gone," West says, his voice cracking a little. He and Alexis had begun to crush on each other, I think. She hasn't talked about him much, but she was always flirting when I saw them together. They must have been closer than I thought, because he looks heartbroken.

"I'm so sorry, West. I should have fought to keep her here, but I was so scared that she was going to die. The medic said that she would be in therapy for at least the rest of this year's cycle; the memories of the shutdown are supposed to be really traumatizing to the victim. I feel like it's our fault because we wanted her to continue the fast. I'm going to miss her so much, but what are we going to do?" I pretend to choke back a sob.

"It's not your fault," Faustino says. "She wanted to do it, remember? In fact, the fast was her idea. I can't believe that the fasting idea didn't work, though. The glitch that allowed the complete separation of the mind from the chip must have been fixed. We're back to square one, but there isn't any time to dwell on it. We need to stick together and get out of here as fast as possible."

Wow. I am officially a master at manipulation. Neither of them even blinks at my story. Faustino has already completely moved on. It is all business in his mind, which I suppose is helpful to me because he won't be brooding over Alexis, unlike West, who is a mess at the moment.

"Yeah, but this is harder than I thought. I feel like we lost half of our group, which I guess we kind of did," West says. He continues after a deep breath, "You are right though, Faustino. There isn't anything we can do about it. Now, what did you need our touchpads for, Mira?" he asks, addressing me.

"Well, I was hoping that I could use them for research. I know it seems like I'm moving on really fast, but I feel like we should get out of here as soon as possible so that nothing happens to the rest of us. I also think that I could work faster if I was able to have multiple sets of resources in front of me at the same time," I say. I am practically holding my breath as I wait for their response. West and Faustino nod their consent. Neither of them raises a word in response to my flimsy reasoning. They really must be dejected because my excuse hadn't been very good.

Faustino starts talking. "Mira is right; we need to focus on getting out. Speaking of which, I purchased a few of the tools we'll need to remove the docks earlier today. You guys should come see them. There isn't any point in sitting around here."

"Sure," West and I say in somber unison.

We trudge out of my apartment and start toward the town. We are all silently going through memories of Alexis. For me, the thought that keep coming back is Alexis had been an orphan. Her parents had left her, betrayed her in a sense, when she was young. She had to grow up in the hands of people who didn't truly love her. I can't imagine the sense of abandonment she must have felt. She thought of her parents as despicable, cruel people, and now she probably thinks of me that way. I had acted like them. I traded her in for selfish reasons, because I hadn't wanted to deal with the problems she would cause. I planted more pain in her heart than I realized. My actions most likely tore apart old scars. The growing sense of guilt is really starting to get to me.

I don't say anything as we walk toward Faustino's apartment on the other side of town. We slowly make our way through the streets. It soon begins to drizzle. The gloomy feeling of the overcast sky and now starless night pushes everyone off the streets. We are alone in our mourning journey. Suddenly, we take a turn into an alley between two restaurants. It isn't dirty or nasty, after all this is The Fisk, but it is creepy and dark. I am about to open my mouth to ask what is going on when suddenly Faustino turns and slaps me across the face. I fall to the ground, stunned. My cheek is throbbing from the impact. I start to yell at him. Why had he done that? But West pulls me over and clamps his hand over my mouth. It is a serious sense of déjà vu. The only thing missing is Faustino wielding a chair leg like a maniac.

I criticize myself, this is no time for irony. I watch as Faustino once again walks toward me. I try to wrench myself away, but West holds firm. I glance around. Had they planned this? We are out alone late at night in the middle of town. Everyone is most likely tucked away in their apartments while I am stranded in the rain. Faustino looks furious. His face is contorted into a mask of pure rage. His eyes are alight, and his neck tense; he looks like he is trying hard to control himself. He isn't doing a very good job though. He has already slapped a girl. His manners could use a little touch up.

Focus, Mira!

I could be facing an imminent death, but it figures that all my brain knows how to do is pull out witty side comments that aren't even funny.

West's hand is like iron over my mouth. I can't speak or move my head more than an inch. Not that it matters though; I am too far from any other living soul for anyone to hear me over the rain. Yes, it figures that the drizzle would turn into a full-out storm. Faustino continues to slowly approach. My brain is working double-time trying to figure out a way to get out of there. I'm not sure why they were doing this, but at the moment I don't really care. My instincts to flee are overwhelming.

"We know what you did, Mira," Faustino says.

What do they know? The only thing I can think of is betraying Alexis, and if they know that, I am done for. I want to ask him what he means but West's hand remains pressed over my mouth. Then

Faustino starts talking again, although I can barely hear it over the pounding rain.

"Yeah, that's right," he accuses. "West saw you talking to that officer. He even heard exactly what you said as you stabbed your best friend in the back. I sent him over to let Alexis and you know that we would have to change our meeting time because West and I had a huge project lined up. He was on his way when he saw you talking to an officer. Then, from inside a nearby store, he watched as Alexis was carted away to who knows where. Lucky I sent him over when I did, or we never would have caught you. You flat out gave Alexis over to the officials. We trusted you, and even let you in on our plans. We came over to your little meeting and sat there as you lied to our faces. I can't believe you did this. You don't deserve to leave the city now, or even live, but since we can't kill you without getting in trouble ourselves, we are going to work out a little deal. West is going to take his hand off your mouth. Now, don't scream or I'll hit you again, and this time it's going to hurt."

No, no, no, nononononononononono. How could this have happened? I hadn't wanted it to come down to this. Karma. It has to be. I had betrayed a friend, and now my friends are betraying me. Whoever said, "What goes around comes around" knew what they were talking about. West peels his hand off my face and pushes my knees out so that I collapse on the wet pavement. Faustino is glaring down at me, furious at what I have done. Behind his head, the rain pours, and the angry, dark clouds reflect the mood.

"Guys," I start. "I'm so, so sorry. She was dying and I had to help. I . . ."

Smack.

Again, Faustino's hand comes ripping across my cheek. It stings so badly I want to cry. Maybe tears will help my case. *No*, I resolutely tell myself. *No more manipulation. Just tell them the truth.* Faustino and West are standing there, waiting for me to continue.

"Alexis was sick and dying, and I tried to talk her out of her fast but she wouldn't listen. She got mad, and I feared that if she told you guys I wouldn't be able to break out of the city with you.

So I told one of the officers about her, not the rebel part, just that she wouldn't eat. I led him to her, and he took her away to get medical attention. Then I . . . came to our meeting," I spit out the hated words, and they leave a bad taste in my mouth. "Why did you play along while we met in my room if you already knew? Were you messing with me?" I ask.

"We were giving you the chance to tell us the truth before we forced it out of you," West says. He still looks heartbroken and furious. Maybe something really had been going on with him and Alexis.

"She was our chance out of the city, and you ruined it for us. You're going to have to pay," Faustino tells me.

"Wait, I'll . . ." I start, but I stop when Faustino threateningly raises his hand as though to hit me again.

"You have one option," he begins. "And you're lucky we are even giving you that, so listen closely. You turned Alexis in, and we never got to see whether or not the fast would actually work. Alexis said she felt her mind detaching from the chip, but because of you, we never got to see for sure if she was right. You are going to purchase the transfer to a new, real body and pick up where she left off. You will not be able to leave your room once the transfer is complete. West and I will bring you water, limited amounts of food, and any other necessities. Other than that, you will remain on lockdown in your apartment. We will run the experiment to its end. Either it will work, or it won't. If not, we'll just have to see what happens."

"What!" I exclaim, temporarily forgetting that they have the upper hand and I am at their mercy. "That's so stupid! Idiotic! Alexis fasted for a full month and nothing happened. If it were going to work, it would have happened a long time ago. That idea was a failure. The doctors must have fixed the glitch. Did you think they were going to leave it be? No, of course not. We need a new plan."

"*We?* Ha! No. Faustino and I need a new plan. You are our little test subject, or worker bee if we need money. You took away Alexis's chance at freedom, and now we are doing the same to you," says West.

I have never seen him this angry. His face is red and there is pain and ferocity in his eyes. Guilt claws and scratches in my stomach, but at the same time, there is anger. I don't deserve this. I was helping Alexis. She had been sick and dying, and I most likely saved her life. She can't be furious for that. These two thickskulled guys are trying to force me to do what they want, but that isn't going to happen. I'm Mira Cobbleson, not some little kid that can be pushed around.

"No," I say confidently as I stand up to face the guys. Faustino swings out his hand to slap me, but I nimbly duck and back away a few steps. I couldn't run because they could always find me again. I have to settle this. "What are you going to do, Faustino? Try to slap me to death? That's not a very good negotiation technique," I taunt. "You can't really hurt me. It would draw too much unwanted attention. Believe it or not, I still don't want to leave our alliance, but you two clearly don't want me. I could always threaten to tell the officials about your plans, but, unfortunately, you could drag me down with you. It works both ways though. If you get me arrested, I can do the same to you. Then none of us will get out. I want to leave the city with you guys, and soon, but you aren't going to use me and then leave me behind. You know you need me. I have most of our money under my name because I have done the most work. I am the only one of the three of us that isn't already recorded as having resisted the Shift. The smartest of the three of us is clearly me, and if any one of us is going to find a new way out, it's me. I know you guys are furious about Alexis but seriously . . . *Oof.*"

Again, I am cut off with a sharp blow. The wind goes rushing out of me as West punches me in the stomach. "I'm so done with you," he says as he steps closer and punches me again. I fall over onto my side on the wet ground and try to shout reason at them.

"You can't do this! The officials will find out and you'll never be able to leave the city. *Aahh!*" I suddenly scream. A searing pain shoots through my core as Faustino drives his work boot into my side. The hard, rubbery plastic drills into the bone of my hip and creates a sensation like getting shot. A kick to the ribs, a fist to the jaw, being yanked up and then thrown back down into the puddle of bloody water that had accumulated where I had been. A bloody and cruel cycle of pain and hurt repeats endlessly in that alley. I go limp as they beat my shell again and again. I feel like a rag doll being tossed back and forth. Faustino's fist to my nose as West holds me up by my hair makes me scream out in agony and terror. No one can hear me though. We may as well have been in the middle of nowhere for all the good my increasingly desperate cries do me. Finally, West picks me up by my battered shoulders and with a look of disgust at my bloody and bruised face, he throws me to the ground. My head snaps back on the pavement.

Blackness. Peaceful, painless blackness.

CHAPTER 12

I wake up in the middle of the night still in that same rainy, dark alley. All I can think about is the hurt. Every thought revolves around the pain I feel. I don't want to move, but I don't want to stay in my little alley. However, pain, coupled with an utter lack of caring, keeps me there. I end up drifting in and out of fitful sleep. Not fun. In between those periods of rest, I think about death, depressing topic I know, but I'm not exactly feeling chipper as I lay there in a puddle mixed with my blood.

You see, even with all the technology available—the identity chips, docks, and medicines—people can still pass away. It is unlikely, but if your shell dies, you are dead forever. Your identity chip can be placed in other living bodies but nothing will happen. The memory of dying, according to doctors, is so powerful it ends the memory making process. Life has always been that way. You are your memories, they say, and if you die in your memories, you are dead forever. No amount of science could reverse it.

In regards to myself, I have no desire to die. Despite everything that has happened, I still don't want it to come to that. The pain awakens something within me that I suppose even a shell has a desire to live. Being broken and battered there on the ground only makes me want to get up and fight back. Life is not going to slip out of my grasp.

Alexis had said, and I had repeated, "Fake life or no life, they are basically the same to me." It had made sense at the time, but now looking back, I was wrong. Trust me, it pains me to say that, but it's true. Life in The Fisk may be unjust, cruel, and fake, but it is life, and there is nothing that compares. Don't get me wrong; I still want out, yearn for it even, but I suppose that "want" no longer rules my life. Desire should never be something that controls you, ever. If it does, it takes away the joy of the little things. If a free life is something I want then, heck yeah, I'll do anything I can to break out, but that doesn't mean the life I have is equal to death.

Alexis had been so focused on anger and escape that she forgot to look around every so often. She had been unable to see the little joys. The things that keep you fighting, like a little bird on its nest, food so good you can't shove it in your mouth quickly enough, and the camaraderie of working together with people you might grow to know and cherish the rest of your life. These things are glimmers of hope that remind you, no matter what, that life is never bad all the way through. That is the thought that keeps me going all through this retched night.

Sleep. Pain. Sleep. Pain. The sequence wears on for hours. I don't know exactly when it happened, but at some point, relief came. An emergency vehicle with flashing lights wakes me up. I am gently placed onto a hovering stretcher and pulled into the car. I want nothing more than to return to the peaceful oblivion of rest. I close my eyelids, dulling the brightness of the harsh lights above me, and I quickly fall asleep.

CHAPTER 13

One would expect, in an advanced society such as our own, that after being recovered from an alley in the middle of the night you would awake to the feeling of numbness. Medicines nowadays can dull or eliminate almost any pain. So why do I hurt so much? My back, face, stomach, and every other part of me throbs incessantly. Thanks, doctors. Or if for some crazy reason they had run out of painkillers they could have at least transferred me to a new body. Ugh, why am I still in this piece of roadkill?

I can hear people talking softly around me, and the light behind my eyelids is still much too bright. I can't sleep, but I really don't want to have to get up and do anything. Being the sweet little angel I am, I decide not to announce my awakening and eavesdrop on whoever was in the room. Maybe I can figure out why they have so cruelly decided not to give me any pain relievers.

"So who is she, and what actually happened to her? She looks pathetic," says a female voice.

Thanks, random person, for that acute observation. Being attacked and beat up by two guys will do that to you.

"Her name is Mira, according to her identity chip ID number. We found her in an alley toward the center of town last night," replies another woman.

"What?" the first lady exclaims. "Why was she there?"

"We are still working on finding an exact reason, but it turns out she was part of a group trying to leave the city. I think she was also the one that turned in that other girl, the one that starved herself."

"So did her getting beat up have anything to do with what happened earlier?" asks the first woman.

"Mr. Walder has someone looking into it. My personal opinion is that the two guys who beat her up thought that she was spying on them from the start. I don't know that for sure, but it seems like as good an explanation as any," replies lady number two.

Who is Mr. Walder? I remember the name, but I can't place it. After a moment of thought, I realize that they must have been referring to Anthony Walder, the tenth generation supervisor. He is the most important guy in the city and now he is involved in this?

Oh, crap. Suddenly, my super slow brain realizes that they also said something about me being a part of the rebel group. How do they know that? More importantly, what is going to happen to me?

"I personally find it kind of funny that they thought they were going to get away with it. It seems everyone thinks that no one is really watching what they do. Little do they know, we monitor everyone in the city. It's even our job title—civilian life monitors."

So we never would have gotten out? The authorities had known what was going on the whole time?

"Ha, they have no idea. AG citizens are so oblivious and naïve."

"Very true. So what is going to happen to Mira here?" It is lady number one again. "She was part of the little escapers group, but at the same time, she was a victim. Will she be treated like a prisoner or a patient?"

"I'm not sure, but I have a hunch that she isn't going to be going back to The Fisk. What she went through was traumatizing, and data from the dock shows that she had a hard time adjusting in the beginning. They may dispose of her card, or take it out of the rotation. Then we wouldn't have to worry about her stirring up a bigger problem in the future, but it's not my decision. It's all up to Mr. Walder."

"Makes sense."

They are going to dispose of my card. I am going to die without ever dying. I can't lie here and take it anymore. I abruptly sit up and open my eyes. Both of the women jump back and let out startled cries. They hadn't known I was awake after all. *Ha, take that, you stuck-up civilian life monitors.*

One of the ladies runs over to a speaker on the wall and pushes a button.

"Mira is awake, sir," she says into the device.

Suddenly, there is a sharp pressure on my arm. The other woman had grabbed a syringe and pressed it into my arm. I try to pull my arm away but her other hand keeps my arm firmly still. It happens so fast. The syringe is already empty, and I am still sitting there on the hospital bed trying to figure out what is going on.

"That should keep you calm," she says.

I panic; I don't want to be calm. Every bloody and bruised cell in my body wants to run. Suddenly, I feel a wave of tingles sweep over my body, and my desires fade into the background. The instinct arises that it is time to make a sarcastic comment but nothing comes to mind. All I can think about is the pleasant feeling that comes over me.

This is so nice. They should have done this before I woke up. My mind drifts through happy thoughts. I can still think clearly but nothing bothers me anymore. Everything is just . . . nice.

I lay back down and listen as Anthony Walder's voice comes through the speaker. "Go ahead and send her in," he says.

The two women walk over to me and tell me to stand up and walk with them. I shakily get up. Luckily, the medicine that had been in the syringe quieted all my pain. I'm sure if it hadn't I would be in a world of hurt as I try to walk. As soon as I gain my balance, the two women take their posts in front of and behind me. Both ladies are dressed in navy green button-down shirts with the letters CLM emblazoned over their hearts. I assume it means citizen life monitor. We walk out the door of my little hospital-like room and head down the hall. The lights are bright and the feeling of the place is very professional and industrial. As we approach the end of the hall, we take a right and head into some smaller corridors lined with offices. I see nameplates with people and positions I have never even heard of before. Angie Goldston is a generation stability officer, and Rudin Sarce is an intergenerational manager of awakening procedures. I'm not sure what all the titles mean, but it does show me that there is a lot more going on behind the scenes than everyone thinks.

We pass quite a few offices before reaching one at the end of a corridor. I see the plaque on the wall that states: Anthony Walder, Tenth Generation Supervisor. One of the two unnamed ladies who escorted me there knocks on the door. Not a moment later, Mr. Walder himself opens the door and pulls me in. The two women left and I am alone in the office with my generation supervisor. The office is large and ornate. Dark lacquered wood bookcases and an immense desk take up most of the room.

"Hello, Mira," he says.

"Hi, um, Mr. Walder?" I replies, not exactly sure what to call him. I can feel the tingly feeling from the medicine starting to fade and my pleasant thoughts go with it. It was nice while it lasted.

Mr. Walder walks around and closes the door. Then he sits down in his large desk chair and says, "Please, call me Anthony. So tell me, how are you doing?"

"Well, Anthony, I feel fantastic," I say dryly, "and I know I look it too." Yup, my good mood disappears with the medicine, and it is rather pathetic because the effects lasted only a few minutes. What kind of scientists developed that?

My sarcasm doesn't faze him. "You had quite a nasty night, didn't you? We want to help you move past that, all of that," he says pointedly, most likely talking about my involvement with a rebel group.

"I don't know what you're talking about." Cliché or not, I am going to play dumb. I have no intentions of turning over any previously unknown information.

"We both know what I'm talking about, but I'll share my take on it." Without waiting for a reply, he continues, "When you woke up here in The Fisk, you had some trouble adjusting. Then you met Alexis, West, and Faustino and joined up with them to try to escape our beautiful city. Your plan involved Alexis starving herself to separate her mind from the chip. However, you saw that Alexis was dangerously starving so you turned her in. Then Faustino and West got mad at you after you lied to them, and they beat you up."

There goes my plan to play dumb. He already knows everything. Anthony leans back in his chair and gives me a chance to reply. I shake my head and shrug my shoulders. He knows he is right, so why try to deny it?

He then continues, "You might be wondering how we know that, but don't worry. I'm going to enlighten you. You see the docks do so much more than hold your memories in your body. In fact, they track many different things. A GPS functions to monitor location, obviously. An audio recorder tracks and stores everything you say. There is even a health-watch system that makes sure your shell is functioning properly. Speaking of shells, did you happen to know that Alexis was in one?"

This is new information. Anthony must have seen my surprise because he gives a haughty little smile before continuing. "Yes, although it's not your fault for not recognizing it. Certain shells are purposely grown with minor flaws to look like real bodies. We had to tell people that their bodies had a chance of being used in the future to keep the peace. However, the real bodies didn't cope as well with the transfer of memories as the shells so we decided to dispose of them and fake it. There were other reasons we didn't use them, but you don't need to worry about that. We are here to decide your future."

"What are you going to do to me?" I ask. I am tired of this stupid show of knowledge and authority.

"This is a difficult topic," he starts. "You wanted to remove your dock and leave the city, which is breaking the law. We can't have that. However, you were also a victim of your actions to try to save Alexis. She is all right, by the way. Your crimes are serious, though. You did play a part in encouraging the dangerous fast and you plotted to leave the city. The typical punishment would be to remove you from the rest of this cycle and the next, meaning that you would be put into hibernation mode until the third year. If your actions had been even more extreme, we were prepared to remove you from the cycles permanently. However, I don't want to do that."

"Not that I'm complaining," I say. "But why not?" He had planned to put me to sleep for a year and a half, wait, nineteen and a half years if we are counting other generation years, but he changed his mind. How kind of him. But why?

"Your generation has been the first with any issue like this. If I enforce that punishment, it will go onto the city records, and I might be downgraded to a lesser job. This, of course, is unacceptable considering how much this generation loves me. It would be a shame to let them down." He flashes another perfect smile.

"You want to keep your title," I conclude, ignoring all of his flowering comments and jumping straight to the point. *What a great guy.*

"Of course I do. Which is why you aren't going into hibernation mode. You are staying awake."

"What?" This one syllable seems to be all that my shocked brain is able to come up with.

"You are going into solitary confinement for a month. At the end of that month, if deemed cured of your rebellious ways, you will be released. Then you will continue to live here in the City Control Center under supervision until we are sure you are safe to release back into society. This will take, at minimum, the rest of your cycle; you will finish out the year here." Anthony finishes dictating my sentence with a cruel smile, but he says it as though he was ordering a meal. The casual and indifferent tone of his voice hints that he is a little more desperate to keep his job than he seems. He is willing to give me a sentence that is deserved by psychopathic murderers.

"But what if I continue to make 'rebellious plans'?" I challenge, mocking his words. I put on a tough face, but underneath I am scared and angry. Solitary confinement was a big-deal punishment before the Shift, reserved for only the most dangerous of people. Even then, it was only used in week-long increments. It could tear someone apart. A month of it . . . terrifies me.

"Then we will remove your chip from the cycles," Anthony threatens. He is cutthroat. It is survive the sentence or die.

"Isn't this extreme? I didn't hurt anyone, and I promise I never would." I am getting frantic. Visions of sitting in a padded, white room knowing there is no way out flashes through my head.

"That was pre-Shift. The most volatile of offenders now are those who disturb our perfect utopia here in The Fisk, and you did that, Miss Mira Cobbleson."

"What about Faustino and West? Alexis?" I asks. "What about them?"

"Alexis is in the same boat as you, so you know you will have a friend going through the same thing. Isn't that comforting? As for the boys, I think I'll increase the artificial infatuation levels in their shells. I can arrange for that, you know. It will make it even easier for them to fall in love with The Fisk. Your dear rebel friends will love it so much that they won't want to leave. Wouldn't that be, hmm, helpful? After all, any more disturbances or crimes, and I might lose my job. Now come on. It's time to go," Anthony says. He stands up and starts walking toward the chair I have been sitting in.

"No! No!" I shout. I stand up and rapidly back up, accidentally knocking over my chair. Anthony changes his course and walks over to a speaker in the wall like the one in my hospital room. He says something I can't quite discern, and a few moments later, two uniformed Fisk officials come in and pick me up by the arms. I kick and scream, but to no avail. They drag me out another door and through the halls. I cry and beg for another chance, but no one listens. I am pulled up to a set of stairs that make my already bruised and bloody legs groan in pain. I try to get my feet under me, but my tears blur my vision, and the guards are moving too quickly. The saltiness of the tears sting as they hit the split in my lip.

By the time we reach the chambers where the confinement rooms are located, I have cried all the tears I had. I watch with a shaking jaw and crazed eyes as Anthony uses his thumbprint to unlock the white door. My bare heels try to dig into the stone floors, but I have no traction. They toss me in, and, before I can even turn around to watch, the door slams shut behind me. I am officially in solitary confinement.

CHAPTER 14

Day one, I do nothing. After the guards leave me in the confinement room, I curl up in a ball on the floor and don't move. For a long time, I rock back and forth and relive over and over the horrible things that had happened. The most recurring scene is the event in the alley. West holding me back like a set of shackles while Faustino struck the first blows. I had no idea that the two of them could be cruel. I have come to realize, while I am in that round little room, one of my biggest flaws is that I am too trusting. I had deluded myself into thinking I was more than a convenient ally to Alexis, and that it was me that Faustino and West valued, not my money. This trust blinded me to what was really going on.

I have no sense of time in that room, but it slowly drifts by. I can't tell when it is night or day because there are no windows. Meals come irregularly. At least, I think they do. I can never keep myself awake for any length of time. At first, I think there is hope. I have to find a way out. Surely there are hidden cameras in the room to monitor me. I spend hours talking out loud, trying to explain myself and beg for mercy. Each time I start, I end in tears because no one comes.

"Please, please, don't let me stay in here any longer," I yell to no one with my hoarse and scratchy voice. "I promise I will be a good citizen, just like Will, just like Will," I end with a whisper. I know I will have no rescuer though. In fact, no one in the entire city of The Fisk cares for me, not enough to save me anyway.

The room itself is a small circle with no furniture at all. I sleep in the middle of the floor on the carpet. The padding on the walls have regular seams and each gap is roughly the size of a door, so I can't remember where the real door had been. It is probably a good thing though, because otherwise, I would have spent all my time banging on it. The only thing that allows me to keep my bearings is a small bathroom off to the side. I try to use the microscopic sink to bathe myself, but I quickly realize it is useless and give up.

I finally abandon my hope that someone will come and find me. I challenge myself to rethink everything that happened after the Shift. I want to hate it, and I do already hate it, but I want to discover so many things that were cruel and evil about it that there will be no light in the picture that comes to mind when I think of the Shift. The little hints of happy memories about life there make me angrier. I am so furious at what has happened to me that I can't stand to think a good thing about that beautiful, wretched city and its twisted lifestyle. I think of the families it ripped apart. The hard earnings that it stole. You aren't in your real body; you are in a replacement, grown on a shell farm. The Shift allows people to hide from their past and make new, fake ones. These people shouldn't be allowed to hide and ignore their past. So many questions arise in my mind in that padded room. I wonder how there are so few protesters when there is so much wrong with this lifestyle. Why couldn't families stay together? Why did they have to be broken up? How did certain people escape the AG lifestyle under the pretense of caring for it? *Anthony Walder, you lying, cheating oppressor. You and all your worker bees shouldn't be able to sleep at night for what you have put people through.*

One thought that haunts me is of children. Alexis had brought up that no one knows where all the children had gone. At the Shift, the kids had their memories uploaded onto the chips like everyone else—even the babies had. What had happened to them though? They weren't old enough to function well in society, but the city designers had to have a program to allow children to grow up. Right? I have a sinking feeling that if they did, we would have heard about it on the Shift advertising campaigns. How has no one thought of this before? Have we been brainwashed? Where have all the children gone?

These are the questions that never leave my mind. Day in and day out, I lie there, driving myself crazy with dark thoughts, and sleep. It feels like I have been here for years, and, who knows, maybe I have.

Then finally, one day, the door opens.

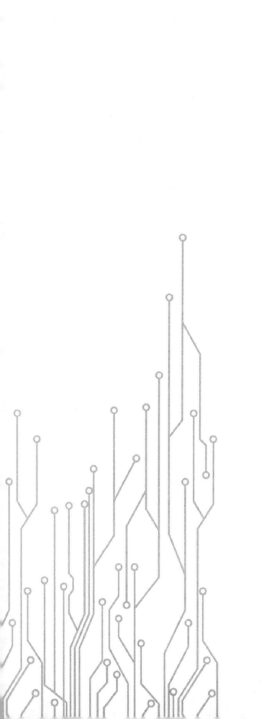

CHAPTER 15

"Hey," is all she says. Leaning against the doorframe is Alexis of all people. She still looks sickly thin and her dirty blonde hair has become stringy and scraggly, but at least she is alive. We have both survived the confinement.

"Hi," I reply, my voice scratchy and hoarse from not talking for weeks.

"Let's get out of here," she croaks out, sounding exactly like I do. I need no further encouragement. I pick myself up and stumble after her. We walk for a long time and see no one.

"Are you sure we are supposed to be doing this?" I ask. The last thing I want is to go back to that cursed room. It has turned me into a grandma. I can only walk slowly and my eyes hurt from the bright lights. My bones ache, and all I want is to sleep.

"We're fine," she says. We walk and walk and walk. There is silence between us, but it isn't uncomfortable. I think we both feel odd talking to another person after having been alone for so long. Not to mention the fact that I had sold her out for my own evil purposes. But all that feels like so long ago, like a hazy and colorful dream. Everything is gray now. Not a happy gray or a sad gray, but merely a state of being.

We finally see other people. We trudge past them, and they don't give us so much as a second glance. Apparently, everybody knows of the failed rebels from Generation Ten, and they don't care about us at all. There aren't any looks of mockery or scoffs of contempt, but instead we are treated like we aren't even there. At this point, I don't even care enough to wonder why.

We descend twelve flights of stairs, and I continue to follow Alexis like a puppy. Eventually we reach a massive gray door. It is tall and imposing and is engraved with the words "THE SILENCED VAULTS." Alexis presses her thumb to a scanner, and the door slides apart smoothly and silently. *How did she get clearance to do that?*

As the crack between the doors grows, I can hardly believe what I see. Wait, that's a lie, I believe it fully and undoubtedly. There are rows of shelves across the entire expanse of the cavern. They stretch upwards more than three times my height, and they run all the way back to the rear wall of the cavern that seems miles away. On the shelves are little black squares no bigger than walnuts—identity chips.

Before me are the silenced. Alexis doesn't even have to explain. The thousands of identity chips stacked on glistening silver racks filling the dark cavernous room belong to the children. I step forward. My bare feet slap against the stone floor and send an echo through the gaping mouth that imprisons the young. I look over at the girl who brought me there. Like me, weariness sweeps over her. Our tired eyes scan the vast room. I find myself walking toward one of the shelves. I press my hand against the cool, hard glass and watch as my breath causes it to fog up. I trace the letters *R*, *I*, and *P* into the fog before it fades. My little brother is in there somewhere. I try to dig my nails into a crack and pry off a piece of glass. It is no use. There is no budging it.

I slowly turn away, keeping my eyes on the cases as long as I can. When my eyes finally disconnect, I feel a tear slide down my cheek. I angrily swipe away the tears. Cane never deserved this. No one could ever deserve this oblivion.

When I look back, I see Alexis climbing one of the twenty-foot cases of chips toward the middle of one of the rows. She looks over and motions with her head for me to join. My safety no longer concerns me. I find myself going up, hand over hand, up the coffins of the memories of the dead. When we reach the top, I look around again. I can see almost every set of shelves.

"Why?" I ask Alexis.

"We wanted to know, remember?" she replies. She is right. At that very first meeting, we had decided we were going to find out what happened to all those who had been too young to function as an AG citizen. Now I know. They had been silenced.

"How did you find me?" I ask.

"I was let out a week before you because I needed the IV drip again."

"You wouldn't eat?"

"Nope." That is a hint of the old Alexis who wouldn't take instruction from anybody. Rebel to the end.

Soon, Alexis is speaking again. "Well, I was let out, and I was taken to talk to Anthony as soon as they got the drip in my arm. He told me that we were essentially stuck here for who knows how long. I told him I didn't care and got up and left his office, pulling my IV with me. After they took me off it on the third day, I started wandering around and eventually made my way here. No one stopped me. I don't think they even care about us anymore, Mira. As long as we aren't in the city disturbing their perfect order, they don't care what we do. I started learning. I found a book, a real book, which contained the entire, complete plan for the AG lifestyle. Did you know that everyone is in a shell? Even me."

I nod, and she continues.

"In that book, it also talked about how they planned to keep the population steady, with no death, but also no birth. Shells are grown to have a chemical imbalance in them that keeps them from wanting to reproduce. The desire is completely gone. No one will ever have children. Mira, these kids all around us will never live. They were never going to be allowed to, but no one would think twice about it. Shells are designed to avert angry thoughts. It's another chemical thing that makes it harder to get angry and stay that way. We are even programmed to love the city like a long-lost home. We were *programmed,* like machines."

Everything she reveals to me makes sense. She is confirming thoughts I hadn't fully formulated but that have been floating in the back of my mind. I remember how easy it was to fall in love with the city, how much I had wanted to love it. It is all programming. It seems so distant now.

"Then that week was over, and I went to get you. I had to ask permission from Anthony, but he said yes. He knew I wasn't going to do anything. He treated me like a servant whom he was graciously granting a gift. It sickens me, but I was allowed to get you as long as I was the one that told you everything about how life here is going to be. Did you know he even installed an electric fence mechanism on our docks that prevents us from going outside? We could get hurt, he says, and that would cause him to lose his valued position as tenth-generation supervisor."

"We should get hurt then," I blatantly state. I don't care about myself anymore, and heck, if it causes Anthony to drop even the slightest bit in rank then it is worth it.

I watch my newfound friend place a small black device on the surface in front of me and say, "That's what I was thinking." Alexis smiles a sad and beaten smile, gives me a little wave, and then allows herself to fall off our perch on top of the shelves.

I hear the crunch and know what has happened.

That's not what I had meant by hurting ourselves. I want to cry so badly it hurts, and, more than anything, I want to follow her to the blissful, unknown peace of the afterlife. That isn't my place though. I look down at the device in front of me through watery eyes and try to read the label on the side. I blink over and over before my eyes are clear enough to read the words. It says "Memory Swipe," and below that is a dial that allows for different increments of time. I can choose any number of months that will be erased. I know what Alexis was referring to.

"Fake life or no life, they are basically the same to me," she had said not too long ago. She chose no life, and now gives me the choice. I think she knew I would choose the fake life. I still see the little joys in life, and I suppose that Alexis must have seen some hint of that. She has given me a gift, and I know it. I climb down and lie beside my silenced friend, whose neck bends at an unnatural angle, and select three months from current date on the device. I hold it up to my neck and hear it latch onto the chip. I glance one last time at the red light on Alexis's dock, and take a deep breath. She will not be making any more memories.

I pull the trigger, and everything goes black.

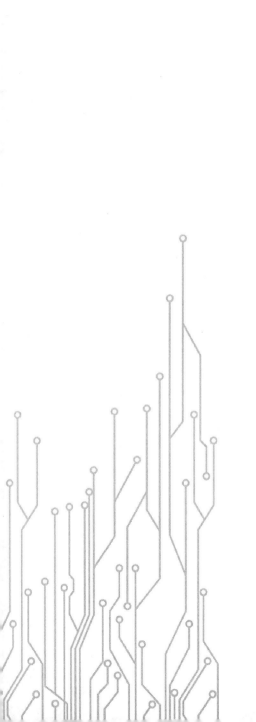

CHAPTER 16

I sweep the long aisles of the vault while whistling my favorite songs from the old days. It is not an ideal job, but a decent one. I am the Chief of Maintenance at the City Control Center. A fancy title for a crummy job, but yup, that is me, Ben Paffter the Janitor.

I have been working at the facility for the entire nine and a bit years it has been open. Pre-Shift, I had been in prison for debt. When the big switch took place, I was offered the opportunity to work for the first full cycle to earn my way to being an AG citizen here in The Fisk. Of course, I took it. My other option had been to allow myself to be silenced forever along with more serious criminals, so the decision was easy.

I had never really agreed with the idea of the Shift, but it got me out of prison, and if a few minds were silenced, I wasn't going to complain. I have learned to accept that there is nothing I can do. Some might say that's selfish, but in reality, it is merely self-preservation.

My current assignment is to sweep The Silenced Vaults, a creepy place. There are machines that could do the work automatically, but they have to give me something to do. So, here I am. Up and down the long aisles I sweep in the semi-darkness of the vaults until I reach about the eighth. While moving my old-fashioned broom back and forth to the beat of the song I am whistling, I look up and see something on the floor. There is a lump, no, two lumps in the middle of the row.

At first, I nearly jump out of my skin, then I run up and immediately stumble back, retching to the side. The two lumps before me are bodies, both girls. Neither is breathing, and the neck of the one girl is bent so far that my own neck hurts looking at it. A moment later, panic sweeps through me. My concern for the two lying there in front of me vanishes. Self-preservation is more important. I could get in huge trouble if I get caught with these shells. I could lose my chance to become a real citizen. I don't know who they are, but I have to get rid of them before anyone sees me.

As carefully as I can, I examine the two bodies. I don't have to look to know that the first girl is dead. The red light on her dock shining through her hair confirms it. The other girl, however, hasn't passed. Her body shows no signs of impact from hitting the ground, but in her right hand is a memory swipe gun still connected to her dock. I reach over to pull the gun from her grasp. Her grip on it is tight, and my hand shakes as I have to pry her fingers off the handle. Horror fills me when I realize that her stiff fingers are still warm. I check her chip, which came out with the device, and see the green light indicating she is still alive but in hibernation mode due to using the device on herself. For a moment, I wonder what brought the two here, but the thought vanishes as my fear of discovery sets in.

I pocket the one girl's chip and take a moment to decide what to do. Dispose of the bodies, a voice in my head tells me. As quickly as I can, I pick up the bodies of the girls and start to drag them to the nearest trash chute. I quickly realize they are too heavy to both be carried at once. I drop the heavier body and cringe as it hits the ground with a dull thud. I will have to come back for it. The chute is a ways down the hall from The Silenced Vaults, and, for the first time, thank the heavens that I have been forced to work late. With a glance down the hall, I see that it is clear and sprint as fast as humanly possible. With each new door I pass, I cringe. Hopefully all the AG officials are as lazy as always and have already gone home for the night. Still, each tiny creak I hear sets my nerves alight.

I make it to the chute without seeing anyone and dash back to the vaults to grab the other girl. She isn't as freakishly skinny as the other one had been, but with the adrenaline pumping through my veins, I don't even notice. I cram her down the chute after the other girl and drop the memory swipe device down after her.

After dumping their bodies and the swipe device, where they would be incinerated in a matter of moments, I rush back to clean up the puke that is on the cold, black stone floor. I pull my undershirt out from under the tan, button-up uniform and use it to mop the mess up as quickly as possible, not caring that there are smears still left on the floor when I leave. The whole time, I am hyped up on adrenaline and fear that someone will catch me and jump to wrong conclusions. They would think I had killed the one girl and swiped the memories of the other. My life would be ruined. I might be silenced for that. I know Walder would silence first and ignore later.

Swallowing becomes a near impossible task. I can't lose my chance at life so close to when I would get it.

I take the chip of the still living girl to the Active Generation Vaults. Those vaults contain the identity chips of the people currently in hibernation. The whole time I struggle to keep my pace normal and a non-freaked-out look on my face. I know I am failing tremendously. When I finally get in, I head toward the closest rotation group to the door, Generation Three. I open the nearest glass shelf and hastily deposit the chip inside and hightail it out of there like the devil himself is after me.

Not knowing what else to do, I go back to the vaults and continue sweeping, terrified the whole time that someone will come in and know what happened.

Yet, no one does. Fortune must have been with me on that fateful night. Years go by, and I earn my citizenship. I never hear anything about that one girl ever again. I suppose she started over—got a brand-new future. It's not like she would have remembered the last one anyway.

CHAPTER 17

I knew it. As I lie on a white bed in a white room with white light filtering in through the shade on the window, I know it has finally happened. The Shift is complete. As soon as I open my eyes, my heartbeat speeds up. I can't wait to go out into the city. I hadn't originally wanted to become an Alternation of Generation citizen, but now, there is nothing I would rather be.

"I'm awake," I say aloud into the tranquil whiteness of the room I am in. Warm feelings spill over me, almost like they came from somewhere else. My entire being feels happy. I waste no time: I get up, change, and head straight out to greet my shiny, new future— my beautiful, beautiful new future.

My first day as an Alternation of Generation citizen is about to begin, and I can't wait.

THE END

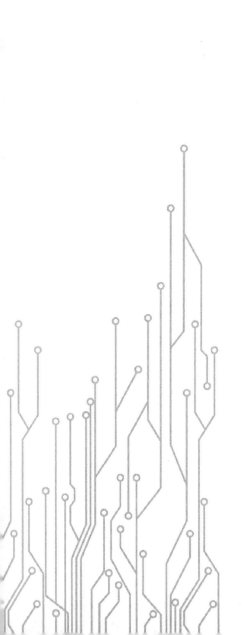

ABOUT THE AUTHOR

H. B. Clementine won the BookLogix Young Writers Contest for *Nothing But Your Memories* at age fourteen while attending Asheville Christian Academy. Now a junior at the nationally recognized North Carolina School of Science and Math, she enjoys writing, playing soccer, and goofing off with family and friends. H. B. Clementine is now creating a series that lights the unsettling path of the Alternation of Generation universe introduced in *Nothing But Your Memories*.

Like H.B. Clementine on Facebook!

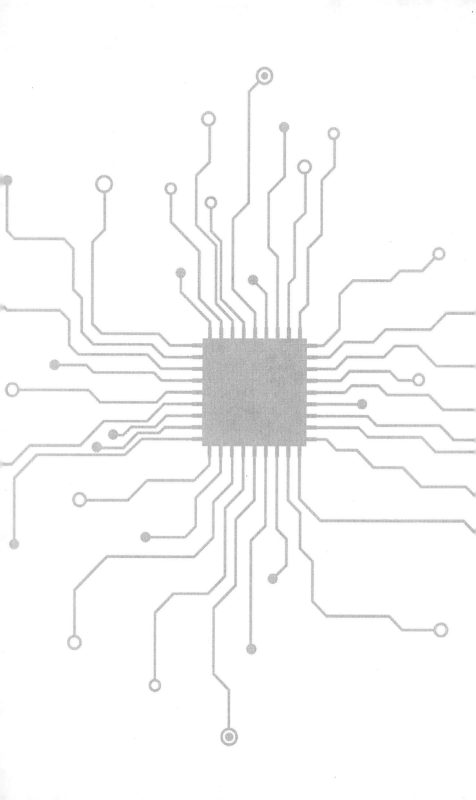